Praise for previous editions

'I can't recall a better collection of multi-authored
short fiction than *New Australian Fiction 2023*.'
—Amanda Lohrey, *Sydney Morning Herald*

'Varied and compelling, showcasing both the state of Australian
writing and the state of the world as seen through it.'
—*Saturday Paper*

'Each story is fresh and boundary-pushing. They refuse to see
Australia through the tired old lenses.'
—ArtsHub

'A sampling of the thoughtful inventiveness exemplified by
our writers, unafraid of shock and disgust, and daring to
experiment with form and style.'
—*Meanjin*

'Writing that fosters intrigue and elicits empathy, deftly
inviting the reader to step into vivid snapshots of moments
in the narrators' lives.'
—*Books+Publishing*

NEW AUSTRALIAN FICTION
2024

Edited by Suzy Garcia

KILL YOUR
DARLINGS

First published in 2024 by Kill Your Darlings
713 Brunswick Street North, Fitzroy North, Victoria 3068 Australia
killyourdarlings.com.au / info@killyourdarlings.com.au

ISBN: 978 0 6454933 4 4 [pbk]

Publishing director: Rebecca Starford
Series editor: Suzy Garcia
Editorial consultant: Darby Jones
Cover design and illustration: Alissa Dinallo
Page design, typesetting and proofreading: Alan Vaarwerk
Printed in Australia by Griffin Press

Kill Your Darlings is assisted by the Australian Government through
Creative Australia, its arts funding and advisory body.

Australian Government

A catalogue record for this
book is available from the
National Library of Australia

The paper this book is printed on is certified against the
Forest Stewardship Council® Standards. Griffin Press holds
chain of custody certification SCS-COC-001185. FSC®
promotes environmentally responsible, socially beneficial
and economically viable management of the world's forests.

Contents

Introduction

Suzy Garcia

L ast year, I did a radio interview to promote *New Australian Fiction*. 'Pretty straightforward questions,' the presenter told me before we started. A few minutes in: 'What makes something *Australian?*'

Oh no, I thought. *Not so straightforward.*

That question makes me think of the GANGgajang song 'Sounds of Then', a favourite of pub bands and Colorbond steel ads. Let's just say I've never been out on that patio. I've never seen lightning crack over cane fields. I've never laughed and thought, *Ah, this is Australia*. At least not in earnest. The fact is, I wouldn't exist if not for the dismantling of the White Australia Policy. Many established notions of Australianness had to change for my migrant parents to come here from different continents, meet each other and produce someone who says *ummm* too many times in interviews.

In the end, I told the presenter that I was not so interested in citizenship or national identity as a necessity for publication. And it's true. We publish writers whose links to this country are varied, sometimes amorphous or ephemeral. After all, in the grand scheme of things, Australia as we know it is a pretty new concept, only made official in 1901. There are First Nations storytelling traditions on this land that reach back tens of thousands of years. The borders have spent more of human history open and porous than they have closed and exclusionary.

But I can recognise that certain texture, that certain beat (look, that song *is* very catchy), that makes our literature distinctive. We all can. In *New Australian Fiction 2024*, the question I was asked in that interview reverberates. Writers push and pull at it to varying degrees. In some stories, Australia is just the backdrop. As everyday as the carpet and walls, as in Erin Gough's 'Dinner Scene', where the Howard years come into focus. It can be a site of uneasy nostalgia in the face of climate change, as in Tracey Lien's 'Goodbye, Blinky Bill'. In others, Australia—the idea, as much as anything else—will never be 'home'. It can be a mirage, as in Kathryn Gledhill-Tucker's 'The Station'. A relic of a distant past, as in Jumaana Abdu's 'Illegal Alien'. Or completely off the page, as in Daley Rangi's 'Black Sand'. And yet every single writer has been shaped in some indelible way by this nation. As a result, it seeps into their stories, and their stories speak back to it.

It shouldn't be a surprise that feelings of unsettlement recur in this book. Recent world events have brought national narratives to the forefront, exposing how a monolithic world view has the power to sever people from a sense of shared humanity. It can be a bind, as conveyed in Behrouz Boochani's 'Qobad'. It can create a hopeless cycle, like the one that we've seen unfold during the production of this book as Palestinians suffer a brutal collective punishment—what the International Court of Justice has deemed plausible acts of genocide by Israel and which is still ongoing. In the words of Ursula K Le Guin in *The Left Hand of Darkness*: 'I know people, I know towns, I know farms, hills and rivers and rocks […] but what is the sense of giving a boundary to all that, of giving it a name and ceasing to love where the name ceases to apply?'

⋅ If there's a throughline in this anthology, maybe it's that our notions of what a country is—and could and should be—are ever-changing. Maybe it's that humanity has never been just about one story but many, and it's important to read it as a collection.

I want to express my gratitude to all the warm and wonderful people who helped bring this book to life. This anthology wouldn't exist without the tireless guidance and advocacy of *Kill Your Darlings*' publishing director Rebecca Starford, who established *New Australian Fiction* in 2019 to provide a platform for fresh local writing and continues to ensure its existence. Further admiration goes to my colleagues Madeline Crehan and Alan Vaarwerk for their hard work and good humour.

To Caitlin McGregor and Mekdes Yimam, our extra submissions readers: I am lucky to have your keen eyes and good taste for stories again! Hats off to the talented Darby Jones—your editorial consulting on the story 'The Station' was inspiring in its generosity and enthusiasm. Cheers to the queen of AusLit book covers, Alissa Dinallo, for our vibrant design refresh. Thank you to Jane Novak, for your kind assistance.

Creative Australia helped fund the creation of this anthology, and we thank them for their support and their championing of Australian literature at large.

To close, a huge thank you to those people who really make this collection what it is:

Thank you to the talented writers who allowed us to feature their brilliant creativity.

Thank you to the supporters of *Kill Your Darlings*, our subscribers and the more than 400 writers who submitted to this year's callout.

Thank you to the booksellers and librarians.

And thank you to the readers—it's for you, it's *all* for you, and we couldn't do it without you!

We hope you enjoy these stories.

Suzy Garcia, series editor
New Australian Fiction
July 2024

Goodbye, Blinky Bill

Tracey Lien

The koalas are disappearing through portals and no one knows why. Sammy listens to the reports on her kitchen radio, reads about it in the news. She sells home-and-contents insurance for Woolworths, doesn't know much about animal behaviour, is used to staying in her lane. But, on the vanishing marsupials, she has her suspicions.

Once a month, Sammy makes the four-hour drive from Fairfield to the Port Macquarie Koala Hospital to volunteer her weekend. They don't need her, but they don't turn her away either. She does it because she likes the coastal drive. She does it because it feels like a grand gesture when everything else in her life feels like it fits in a teacup. She does it because, like most people, she loves koalas and, unlike most people, she has the time.

When the koala numbers begin to dwindle, volunteers and rangers suspect that it's from recent bushfires. They were already down from deforestation, road accidents, dog attacks and marsupial chlamydia. The latest fire season, fuelled by yet another unnaturally dry and unforgiving summer, must have done the rest of them in. But then the rangers in Port Macquarie hear from the rangers in the Blue Mountains that more than a hundred koalas have been found going single file through a koala-sized portal. One second, they're here; next second, *poof*!

The Blue Mountains rangers try getting through too. The University of NSW sends bug-sized robots—the kind with infrared sensors used in search and rescue. Boston Dynamics volunteers the latest iteration of its robotic quadruped, Spot. The portals always close for anything but koalas.

'Thing is,' says Matty, a Port Macquarie volunteer in his sixties who used to teach high-school English, 'do we even know if the koalas are going anywhere?' He pulls freshly laundered towels from the hospital washing machine and hands them to Diane, a retired nurse who started volunteering after she lost her husband of forty years to melanoma.

'Another universe,' Diane says, dropping the towels into a basket.

'Like in *Sliders*?' Sammy asks.

'I'm sorry, hun?'

'*Sliders*,' she says. 'The show from the nineties—'

'I'm afraid I'm too old for that.'

'What if they're evaporating?' says Matty. 'What if they become atmosphere? What if they're neither here nor there?'

Diane frowns.

'I wanna write them a song,' Matty says.

'You should,' says Sammy.

'But I don't know how.'

'I can help you, love,' says Diane. 'My Larry taught music, you know. He taught me a thing or two.'

S ammy begins driving down to Port Macquarie twice a month. Folks wanting to get ahead of koala disappearances start scooping them up from the wild in laundry baskets and bringing them to the hospital. The head vet at Port Macquarie, Dr Lozza, begs locals to leave the koalas alone, that it does more harm than good to ambush a koala for no reason, that a koala will fight back if provoked.

'Stop it!' she pleads when more people bring healthy koalas into the hospital. 'We're a koala hospital, not a koala jail!'

Sammy eavesdrops on the vets as she feeds eucalyptus mush to Barbara, a grey-brown adult koala. The first time they met, Barbara, then an adolescent, had been struck by a Toyota Echo. After being patched up, she was attacked by a dog. During the recent fire season, a firefighter sweeping through a charred swathe of forest came across a tiny lone figure searching for water. Barbara's foot pads had been roasted. Her nose—normally glossy and black—had crusted pink. Patches of fur had been scorched off her body.

'You hear that?' Sammy whispers to Barbara as she brings more mush to the tired creature's mouth. 'Can I tell you my theory?'

Barbara chews. Sammy lays out why she thinks the koalas are leaving, thinking of her parents and how they fled Vietnam. She asks Barbara, 'Have you heard of refugees?'

The koala slow-blinks. Sammy thinks it could mean she gets it. But, then again, everything Barbara does is slow.

T he animal hospitals and wildlife parks grow chaotic. Sammy begins driving to Port Macquarie every weekend to take up bandage-changing and mush-feeding duty for sick and injured animals while the other volunteers talk civilians out of kidnapping koalas from the portal lines and keeping them in their homes. The parks, nature reserves and clinics have never been better funded after an outpouring of donations. But for once they don't know what to do with it. Physicists can't figure out why the gateways formed or where they lead. Animal psychologists don't know what's causing the koalas to leave.

A portal appears inside an enclosure at Australia Zoo. The Irwins, seen holding koalas Margie and Bill, sob: 'We'll let them go, if that's what they want.' The federal government, fearful of what this means for tourism, finally decides to talk policy. The prime minister appears on air, belligerent. He blames: the Chinese, the Russians, climate change activists, environmental terrorists, tech giants, the Chinese (again), calls it a hoax, walks it back. A senator from Queensland who has spent her career disparaging First Nations people pens an op-ed in a national newspaper titled: 'Dear Aboriginals—now is the time to do something.' A First Nations elder responds on live TV: 'Dear Senator—now is the time to fuck off.'

'I don't know if I want to live in an Australia without koalas,' Matty confides in Sammy after spending a morning freeing half a dozen koalas from a woman's van. The woman, a kaftan-wearing realtor, had planned on driving the koalas she'd kidnapped from a portal line in Newcastle to Alice Springs, where she was convinced the power of Uluru would keep them safe. The woman was not aware that koalas can't survive in the desert. 'I mean, what does it say about us if we can't even save something so precious?' Matty drops his head. 'When the world looks at us, what will they see?'

S itting in her childhood living room, cups of tea between the three of them, Sammy and her parents watch a morning show host interview two mammologists who are at odds on what to do about the koala crisis. As the mammologists are introduced, infographics appear across the screen: *Around the time of federation, humans shot and killed eight million koalas for their pelts. In a single month in 1927, eight hundred thousand koalas were killed, turned into gloves and hats.*

Recently, the news bulletin reports, the official nationwide koala count was just under two hundred thousand. Although today, post portals, no one can be sure if that figure is accurate.

'Why would anyone do that?' Sammy's mother says in Teochew. 'Shooting a sleepy animal for fur? Shameful. If a koala wanted to live in our mango tree, I would allow it.'

Sammy's parents are both retirees who spend their days in their home highlighting deals in shopping catalogues, tending to their tropical fruit trees and watching *Paris By Night* and *Asia* DVDs. They prefer the episodes with the old songs, often replaying the ones they heard back in Vietnam. Sammy once asked her father why they listened to the same ones on loop. Her father had thought for a moment. 'It proves that we were there, that our memories are real,' he said. 'It proves that it was home, even if not anymore.'

The mammologists now talk about animal extinction. They talk about the last known Tasmanian tiger, Benjamin, who died alone in concrete and chicken-wire captivity in Hobart, September 1936. They play black-and-white footage of him pacing in his final days. The video is silent.

'I had a dog in Vietnam that looked like this,' Sammy's father says.

'I never knew you had a dog.'

Her father lowers his eyes.

'We couldn't bring the dog when we fled,' her mother says, looking at Sammy's father. 'It was an old dog.'

'We had to leave him behind,' her father says, his eyes now on his cup of tea. He looks like he might cry.

Sammy and her mother decide to give her father privacy by looking away, at the TV. On screen, the two mammologists are in a heated debate.

Camp One: Stop the koalas from leaving. Find space in zoos, wildlife reserves, house them somewhere so that they can't get to a portal.

Camp Two: Let them go. There's nothing that continental Australia has left to offer. The trees are charcoal, the air perpetually choked with smoke. The threats against their lives are unabated. To make them stay would be an act of cruelty.

'Are you asking us to give up on our national icon?' asks Richie, the morning show host.

'No,' says the Camp Two mammologist. 'I'm asking, how much can the koala bear?'

On Sammy's next drive up to Port Macquarie, the frothy blue ocean to her right, layers of jagged rock to her left, the waves inspire a memory, the same memory she's replayed on every drive since the portals opened, the memory that's inspired her theory.

She's ten years old, legs dangling over the armrest of a brand-new recliner. Her parents, faces plump, hair still mostly black, re-enact a story.

'And then I saw a pirate ship riding the waves, coming towards us!' her mother said, on her feet, pointing into the distance. Sammy's eyes followed the line of her mother's finger, landing on a bunch of *Paris By Night* tapes stacked on top of the VCR. 'And I told your father, throw me overboard! I'd rather die than be taken by pirates! Because that was what pirates did back then—they would ambush your boat at sea, kidnap all the women, kill all the men. So I jumped! I jumped off the boat!'

'And I grabbed her because drowning is a terrible way to die,' her father said.

'So now I'm hanging off the side of the boat, telling your father to let me go because I was ready to die, and he wouldn't let go, so I was just dangling there like a sweet sausage! You know the sausage I put in fried rice?'

'Yeah.'

'Dangling, like that!'

'And as I was pulling your mother up—'

'And as he was trying and failing to pull me up, because we'd been at sea for five days—no food, no fresh water—we were so weak, we were going to die, your father had no strength to pull me up—'

'As I was pulling your mother up—'

'The pirate's boat collided with ours and crushed my leg! I went blind from pain! I felt so much pain there was no pain! I was dead but not dead!'

'Turns out they weren't pirates,' her father said.

'My leg! It was broken all over the place!'

'It was another fishing boat carrying refugees that had lost its way.'

'It was broken in four places! Five places! Six places! My leg!'

'And it turns out we were only hours from Pulau Bidong. Once we got there—'

'They said I'd never walk again! They said I might die from having a leg so broken!'

'They let us leave the refugee camp to go to a hospital.'

'I had to learn to walk again!'

'The guards let me sneak out of the refugee camp to visit your mother.'

'It was a miracle!'

'And once your mother recovered, she joined me in the camp, and we had to stay there a full year before resettlement.'

'Miserable! My leg!'

'Then why did you do it?' Sammy asked.

'Do what?' her father said.

'Become refugees. Why not just stay in Vietnam?'

And here her parents—the most youthful she can remember them being, their cheeks still fleshy and smooth, their joints not yet inflamed with arthritis—made her shuffle to the centre of the recliner so they could each take an armrest.

'My daughter,' her father said, resting a hand on top of her head. 'Why do you think someone would risk everything to leave the only home they've known?'

Sammy shrugged. She vaguely knew that her parents had left Vietnam because of communism, but she had never really understood what that meant.

'It's when staying is the same as dying,' her mother said.

'If staying means dying, but leaving means the possibility of something else,' her father said, 'even if you don't know what that something else is, even if you don't know where you'll end up or what will happen to you—'

'Then,' her mother said, leaning in and whispering into Sammy's hair, 'you leave.'

A koala portal opens a hundred metres from the Port Macquarie hospital. Barbara, whose paws are still in bandages, doesn't take an interest. At least not yet. Sammy props her up in a cushioned laundry basket on the hospital's porch. She strokes the koala's soft head before Barbara gives her a lazy look—*That's enough.*

Together they stare at the rustling leaves on nearby gum trees. Sammy hums, to avoid the silence that can swallow a species into extinction. She hums a Kylie Minogue, the theme to *Blinky Bill*, a few from the Backstreet Boys. She hums the Vietnamese songs her parents like from *Paris By Night*—the ones whose lyrics she doesn't understand but gets the gist of.

When Barbara falls asleep, Sammy takes her inside and joins the volunteers on the grassy knoll where the portal glimmers. Matty sits on the ground with a guitar in his lap.

'Turns out I'm pretty useless at songwriting,' he says. 'Not Diane's fault. She did her best with me.' He begins picking the chords to 'Waltzing Matilda'. 'How about I play us a classic instead?'

Diane is crumpled beside him in tears. Dr Lozza stands and stares with her arms crossed. Koalas—dozens of them, full-grown, lone teens, mothers with joeys on their backs—walk at a leisurely pace through a shimmering hole in the air.

Sammy sits cross-legged with her fingers in the grass. She feels her shoulders droop, her face numb. She misses the koalas. She misses them while they're here. She knows she'll miss them even more when they're gone.

Matty starts to sing, those lyrics they all learned in primary school, lyrics about a different time, a different life, but whose melody rings of home. Sammy joins in. Dr Lozza too. Diane fits in song between sobs. They sing to seek forgiveness. They sing to feel less alone. They sing to quash the silence, to bid goodbye, goodbye and good luck, wherever you go.

Rocklands Road

Ceridwen Dovey

A few nights before my surgery, I asked my mother to make me meat dumplings wrapped in cabbage leaves, stewed in tomato sauce. I remembered her making this meal thirty years earlier, on my fifteenth birthday, right before she and Dad left my older sister and me to live alone in the flat on Rocklands Road.

We'd needed to finish high school here. They'd needed to return to their jobs in another country.

Now it seems to me like an impossible emotional equation to resolve, but at the time the decision was made quickly, with stoic sadness. It was a fault in our family's storyline, in service of the future. We daughters (seventeen, fifteen) would live alone in the flat, and our parents would come and visit when they could get leave from work on the other side of the world.

These days, my mother can't stand up for very long to cook because her spine aches, so my dad—who never cooked in over fifty years of marriage—has become her sous-chef. She sits at the dining room table, chopping things, and calls out instructions to him at the stove.

For the dumplings, they bought the last whole cabbage at the grocer. 'People don't eat cabbage much anymore,' my mother said. 'Or they seem to be able to make do with only halves and quarters.'

But for this recipe they needed whole cabbage leaves, which my dad poached in salted water, one by one, until they went translucent. He carefully lifted the sturdy but soft leaves out of the water and laid them on paper towels to dry.

At the table, my mother's job was to stuff the cabbage leaves with the meat filling and swaddle them into little packages, nestled side by side in the baking tray. She remarked that the leaves looked like the caul around a newborn puppy. The sauce was poured over, and the dish went into the oven.

We were unsure if the kids would like this meal, but they ate every scrap. 'Let's call them *dinosaur turds!*' said the youngest.

After we'd eaten, to keep the mood light in spite of what lay ahead, we played a dinner party game where two of us were tied together with string and had to figure out how to detach ourselves.

My parents had learned this game when they were young newlyweds living in France, when my dad was playing rugby for a team in Bordeaux. My mother had taught herself textbook French, but not nearly enough to know what was going on in her job as a physiotherapist. She had to use pulleys and straps to elevate people, some quite elderly, above the ground. French physiotherapy, she used to say, was like being in an arcane, medieval circus school—you never knew when your whole world was going to be tipped upside down or flipped inside out.

There is a trick to getting untangled from your partner in the string game. Everybody focuses on getting their bodies untangled, but actually it's about looping the string under one wrist—in one tiny gesture, you've set yourself free.

When my sister and I lived on our own, it was in a flat my parents had rented in a block on the Pacific Highway, opposite our school. That apartment block is at the top of Rocklands Road. The flat I moved into with my own children, many decades later, is down the bottom of Rocklands Road. After all my peregrinations, I ended up travelling in a circle, returning to the source.

The second-floor flat where we lived as teenagers had a balcony that jutted out the back of the building, facing the apartment complex's tennis court. My sister and I had nowhere else to look but directly into the hospital's glazed windows opposite. We used to wonder if we were looking at the hospital incinerator, where all the hazardous medical waste or biological material extracted from people—tumours, organs, placentas—was burned, because like clockwork, every few hours, smoke would puff out of a vent at the top of the building and be taken away by the wind. It was always white smoke, like a successful papal enclave announcing that a choice had been made.

To the left of the hospital building was a sliver of a view of the distant Iron Cove bridge, but a tree was growing on the hospital grounds, eclipsing it.

On his first visit back to see me and my sister, Dad decided he would trim the tree and reclaim the water view. He found a saw in his toolkit, and one night, after dark, he and I wrapped the saw in a beach towel and took the lift down to street level. We walked along the narrow concrete pedestrian pathway beside the complex's tennis court and the hospital. I stood lookout on the path while he hoisted himself up the green wire fence and hacked away at a few of the branches.

A nurse getting in her car in the carpark looked like she was going to say something, then drove away. It was a mild spring evening, and daylight saving had just begun, and suddenly the streetlights along the pedestrian walkway came on—spotlighting my dad up the tree. He froze mid-saw. I started to sweat. People in our apartment block were silhouetted moving around in their kitchens with the windows open.

'Hold up the towel!' my dad hissed from up the tree.

I had been living with only my sister for several months, and since he'd been gone, Dad had become a loveable, mad stranger to me. He had brought a highly charged energy into the flat, one that I hardly remembered. He'd mucked up our little routines. We were still figuring out how to live together for the two weeks of his visit, and it was day thirteen.

I stood with the beach towel held up under the bright light so my father could climb down the tree he was mutilating. We wrapped up the saw again and went the long way back to our apartment-block entrance.

From our balcony, the sliver of the Iron Cove bridge and pink water was once more clearly visible.

Only after he'd left did I notice that in our haste to get away, we'd trampled a yesterday-today-and-tomorrow bush beneath the tree, with its hopeful triad of blossoms.

The flowers start out purple, then fade to lilac, then fade again to white as they age. Each flower on the bush is ageing at a different rate, so in the spring you will always see all three colours blooming at the same time. Be careful of them though: their roots and petals contain neurotoxins, and are poisonous to humans.

Rocklands Road is only three blocks long once you turn off the highway. There's nothing very interesting about it, except for the hospital.

This hospital is where people come to give birth. It's also where they come to find out about the horrible things growing inside them (not babies) in the basement imaging labs, and to have those things cut out in the surgical wards above. They come for the chemicals that may or may not cure their cancer.

At the top, the street forms a wind tunnel, the wind whistling down from the highway and the truck traffic past the small, human dramas playing out on the pavements. Heavily pregnant women clutch their partners' arms. Elderly couples walk silently side by side, holding oversized envelopes containing X-ray or MRI results.

Sometimes people sit in shock or cry softly on the low brick wall at the hospital's boundary. There is always someone hooked up to a drip and smoking defiantly outside the delivery entrance.

Often, in the early afternoon, pairs of new parents can be seen leaving the hospital, carrying their newborns in brand-new car capsules, the mums hobbling slowly down the hill. They figure out how to clip the capsule into the car seat, the door slams, and off they drive, into the rest of their lives.

The nuns after whom the hospital is named—the Mothers of Mercy—still live in the area, and are well looked after. I know this because I work for the home-visits team at the local library; we drive around delivering books to elderly or unwell people.

A few months ago, we visited a nun who lives in a modern apartment block just up the road from the hospital, to drop off some books and a bag of DVDs of musicals (*Guys and Dolls* and

Hello, Dolly!). She had worked her whole life as a remedial teacher, she told me. She was bright and friendly. For lunch, she was poaching an egg twirled in Glad wrap in a saucepan of water. Beside the pan was a glass jar of onion marmalade; a dollop on top and lunch would be ready. It struck me as an elegant meal.

From her balcony, I noticed that the tree my dad had butchered would have blocked her sliver of the Iron Cove bridge and the changeable waters of the distant harbour too, if its branches had been left to grow.

She followed my gaze. 'I love that view,' she sighed.

I didn't tell her that the man who'd illegally gifted it to her now denies ever having tried to cut down the tree beside the hospital. I mentioned it once to him, laughing about our escapade, and he'd said, 'I never did that.' I didn't argue. He had erased it completely from his memory.

When the wind blew in a certain direction, my sister and I could hear the school bell from across the highway, and we'd leave it to the last possible minute to jaywalk across the lanes of traffic, once with my sister barefoot, holding her school shoes; another time with pieces of toast sticky-taped to my jumper for the Year 11 poetry lunch, where I went as *something horrible on toast*—a line from Gwen Harwood's 'Hospital Evening'.

Gwen Harwood was the poet we were studying in English that year and her poems were layered with all the things I felt about my own family: so much love, and certain pointed, hidden kinds of ambivalence. The poet's daring, in making these word capsules that said it all without explicitly saying *any of it*, was what appealed. The smooth surfaces of life often disappointed me. I was interested in when things ruptured, when masks came off, when inner thoughts were transmuted into external words, when something more authentic broke through. I could see that catastrophes big and small made people briefly more authentic with one another, but then the smooth surface would close over again. Gwen Harwood had found a way to live beneath the surface. I wanted to join her there.

My sister and I were aware that living alone as teenage girls, without parents around, meant we could spend most of our time in our own heads, and do things that were slightly eccentric without being defined by them. Those were the years when I first grasped the deep pleasures of my own company. At home in the flat, while my sister studied late at the library, I wore a long white satin nightie, and sometimes swam night lengths in the apartment complex's indoor pool downstairs whose walls had a creepy hand-painted mural of monkeys dining in an abandoned castle. I made cassette tapes of myself reading out Gwen Harwood's poems, and listened to them on repeat to memorise them.

My sister drove us to Woolies once a week, on a Saturday afternoon, where we did our food shopping together. She did our laundry, and I did all the cleaning and paid the bills, carefully managing the money my parents wired to our bank account. My parents liked to joke that I was the Minister of Finance. My sister ate mostly celery salad—chopped celery, apple, dates, almonds. I ate mostly pasta with tinned tuna and cheese.

My sister and I were diligent about doing our homework at the shared desk in the second bedroom, though nobody told us to do it. Only one mistake was ever made. While on the landline to a friend, my sister forgot she'd turned on the laundry sink tap and flooded the whole apartment. We didn't tell our parents. The rented industrial fans whirred for weeks to get the carpet dry again and the Minister of Finance fudged the accounts that month.

We kept a baseball bat inside the front door, the only acknowledgement of how vulnerable we might be. For a while, my sister dated an older man, a hard, cruel Dane she'd met at a shopping centre, and when she broke up with him, we were both afraid he might try to break down the door.

Several days after the cabbage dumpling dinner, I walked up Rocklands Road to the hospital to have my tumour cut out.

My family, old and new—parents, partner, sons, sister— came with me, and stayed until I was taken away through the swinging doors. Lying on the gurney in a gown and compression stockings, I was trolleyed around the place and eventually left for quite a long time in the surgery ante-theatre, facing the very same opaque windows my sister and I had once stared at on summer evenings.

From inside the hospital, I could see the flat where my sister and I used to live. The blinds were drawn, but somebody was moving around in the flat upstairs from ours, the one that stood empty for a long time after the owner hanged himself in the big underground space beneath the building. That was so long ago now. We didn't see his body, but his garage cage was directly opposite ours. Somebody covered the inside of it with blue plastic afterwards, and we hated being down there in the dark.

As I lay on the gurney, occasionally a tennis ball would arc in a parabola across my view; someone was playing on the court between the hospital and the apartment block.

The anaesthetist was chatty. I told her that I used to live in the apartment opposite, and she looked out the window and said, 'I've always wondered if they can see us in here, like we can see them.'

I almost asked her then if the incinerator in which my tumour would later be burned was nearby but stopped myself: I sensed it would make me seem morbid, even unhinged, to ask such things right before I was about to have my body sliced open.

Instead I told her with solemn authority that no, nobody could see in, not even at night when the hospital lights were on, that all we had ever been able to see were reflections of the tennis court fence and the sunlight and a shimmery mirage of our own apartment, of ourselves. A sliver of water view to the left. A puff of pure white smoke every now and then, curling up into the air, like a sign.

'Of what, peace?' she said, giving me a curious look that made me realise I was going under.

'To signal a decision has been made,' I replied. The tennis ball arced again. The view was finally clear, and I slipped— stoic, sad—beneath the surface.

A Dog's Life

Dominic Amerena

Jan said Japan was where the money was, so that's where we went—Tokyo, to be exact. She rented a penthouse in Akihabara, done up in blonde wood and gleaming chrome. The owner gave me a discount in return for selfies with my dog, Porcini.

We spent our days endorsing steak knives, Thermomixes and delousing shampoos. Photo shoots and promo videos, guest spots in film clips for J-pop bands, drop-ins with reality TV stars: men in silver suits and women in puffy, vaguely Bavarian costumes. I smiled and nodded as the production staff swirled around me.

Jan attached a GoPro to Porcini's collar and set up a subscription service called *A Dog's Life*, which streamed his life to his adoring fans. I never understood what possessed people to fork over ten dollars a month to watch close-ups of Porcini's dinner being wolfed, the darkened apartment as he slept, but fork they did.

Two months in, Porcini began losing weight. He turned his nose up at wagyu steaks, quivering cubes of tuna. Besides the occasional bowl of kibble, he spent all day on his blanket, licking his arsehole. Subscriptions were down and so was Jan.

—Is he depressed? Jan asked. Have you been mistreating him?

—Do I even need to dignify that with a response?

—Well, yes, if you wouldn't mind. Dignify away.

My job, if that was the right word, was simple: I fed Porcini and took the photos Jan suggested. My bank account swelled like a blood-filled tick, but I was finding it harder to get out of bed in the morning. One day I decided to take control. I did ten sit-ups and called Jan.

—I want to be more involved. I want to connect with my fans.

—*Your* fans?

—Ours. His.

—Fans can be tricky. Unpredictable. You know that saying about meeting your heroes? Well, it goes the other way too.

I could hear Jan breathing down the other end of the line.

—I want to meet people. Real people.

—But you're not a real person. Not anymore. And the sooner you realise that the better.

—I want the passwords to the Instagram accounts.

—Now let's not do anything rash. I'm coming over.

She did, all the way from LA. We started on beer, then switched to whisky. She was plying me to weaken my resolve.

—You are the owner of the most famous dog on the planet, Jan hissed. Porcini is your meal ticket, your gift dog, your manna from canine heaven.

But I stood my ground, and eventually she relented. If involvement I wanted, involvement I'd get.

A few days later, I met the inaugural winner of the Pals of Porcini competition, an ESL teacher named Kaitlin, who'd been selected to meet my dog from his 7.7 million Instagram followers. She trembled on my welcome mat in charcoal activewear, her hair dyed a silvery orange. Porcini was asleep on the same tatty blanket I'd taken him home in half a decade earlier. She crouched and hovered her hands above his brindle coat.

—Look at him. Look at him.

I took some photos, but she looked overwhelmed—not good content-wise. I clapped my hands and Porcini began to stir, yawning and licking his chops. Finally he sat up and offered his chin to Kaitlin, which she proceeded to chuck as she murmured solemnly:

—Kawaii. *Kawaii.*

We smoked on the balcony, looking down at the people moving far below on Chuo Dori. Kaitlin had been following Porcini from the beginning, liked all his photos, watched his videos, bought his cookbooks. Silly as it sounded, Porcini held an important place in her heart, she told me. He was a symbol of all that was good in the world.

Kaitlin was from Ann Arbor, a university town an hour's drive from Detroit, raised by her mother, Jill, a receptionist at a doctor's office. They got along well enough, though Jill drank from the moment she got home from work until she passed out on the living room couch. Kaitlin often found her mother in the bathroom, doubled over from the pain in her kidneys.

Eventually Jill decided to give up the booze for good. Kaitlin stayed up with her on those wintry Michigan nights to keep her running to the liquor store. They bought a staffy from the pound, Bruno, a wimp of a thing. They played with him for hours at a stretch, tickling and hugging, smelling the top of his head.

Jill seemed happier, though she worried about the dog. It had terrible separation anxiety, whining pitiably whenever they left. She began driving home during her lunch breaks to spend a few minutes with him. One time Kaitlin got home early from school and discovered her mother asleep on the couch with Bruno whining beside her. Careful not to wake her, Kaitlin tiptoed through to the kitchen and rifled through the cupboards and the trash, looking for empty bottles, but couldn't find any.

Two weeks later, Kaitlin got the call from the hospital. Jill had been in a car crash on the drive back to work. She was in an induced coma with a blood-alcohol level three times the legal limit. Later Kaitlin found the vodka bottles at the back of her mother's closet. Her mother's concern for Bruno had been a cover to drink without Kaitlin knowing. While she waited for her mother to wake up, Kaitlin found she couldn't bear the sight of the dog, and eventually sent him back from whence he'd come: the pound.

After Kaitlin left, I padded around the apartment, eating mechanically from a bag of yoghurt pretzels. I locked myself in the tiny, grey-tiled bathroom. Porcini followed me everywhere, slinking between my ankles, streaming my image to strangers around the world. The toilet was the one place I got to be alone. It was low to the ground, and I always made a mess when I stood to pee, but when I sat there was nowhere to put my legs. I usually went in the shower. While washing my hands my phone buzzed; more messages from Adam Driver.

—*I've been working on my accent.*

He'd sent a few audio files.

—Bloody hell! What's the dog doing at the stove? Adam squawked in a broad Australian brogue.

I sent him a thumbs-up without listening to the rest. He was one of Jan's clients. She had brokered the deal to option my life.

—Adam has big ambitions, she told me. He wants to direct, produce, *innovate*.

A few weeks after the meeting with Kaitlin, we were booked to appear on the most popular cooking show in Japan. I decided on yakisoba for the dish, the most complex we'd ever attempted. In preparation, every morning I'd set out the ingredients on the apartment floor, next to a wok on a hotplate. I'd mime the motions Porcini needed to perform, and he'd wag his tail and lick my hand with fat, dumb love. He'd set to work with a paring knife between his nimble paws, but he couldn't seem to get the ratios right: he used too much pork, he overcooked the noodles, the balance of soy and ginger was all wrong. I worried I was overextending him, that it was a dish too far, but he seemed to relish the challenge, his torpor disappearing the longer he spent at the stove. He so desperately wanted to impress me, to be the good boy, to wring out what little love I had.

One morning I found Porcini alert next to the wok. He was ready.

—I am quivering with excitement, my dude, said Adam Driver, Zoomed in from the kitchenette. I'm beyond quivering.

I put the ingredients on the ground and Porcini got to work. He diced the vegetables into spears, sliced the pork fingernail-thin and dumped the food into the wok shimmering with oil.

I called Jan with the news.

—This is the sound of me kissing, she said. Consider yourself kissed.

I drank celebratory Kirin after celebratory Kirin. I high-fived Adam Driver through the screen. Porcini rumbled around the flat, yapping in delight.

Eventually, yakisoba would be the dish that truly elevated him to the A-list, spawned his Michelin-starred restaurants and the reality TV show, *Canine Kitchen*. Porcini is everywhere now: on *MasterChef* and *The View* and the UN Commission on Animal Rights in the Global South. I've watched his ascension from the gloomy confines of my living room, feeling a mixture of pride, envy and relief.

A Dog's Life has been rapturously received by audiences and critics alike. Porcini praised for his understated performance, Adam Driver for his sympathetic portrayal of me (*a hangdog loser from Central Casting*, as one critic put it). The film has put me back in the spotlight: abusive messages and calls from journalists, all my ex-therapists *reaching out* to offer their services.

E ight years earlier, I'd seen an ad on late-night TV where a corgi vogued at the camera while a Shar Pei rolled in a meadow. The woman at the North Melbourne no-kill shelter greeted me with a watery grin, gave me some forms and coaxed Porcini to the bars of his cage.

—He's had a hard life, she said.

It looks like you have too, I imagined her thinking. Back then I left a silvery trail of sadness wherever I went. My apartment backed directly onto the Barkly Street KFC, resulting in chicken-themed dreams.

—So abject, Adam would say, when I narrated that time in my life. So kitchen sink.

I was working at a call centre, selling gym memberships. One night I returned from a shift to find Porcini plating up an omelette. It was yellow and light, gooey in the middle. Of course I had no idea what had happened. Had I left the stove on? Had a burglar made a snack and forgotten to eat it? But the next day the dog was at it again, and the next day too. Simple, gluggy dishes: risotto, dhal and tuna pasta. I began to film him and uploaded the videos. His name wasn't Porcini back then. He didn't have a name.

The day after the yakisoba triumph, I was mortally hungover. It was just getting dark when Jan rang up from the street. Opening the door, her expression said: *Something terrible has happened.*

—The first thing I want to say is, I'm sorry it had to end like this. The last thing I want to say is, we can do this the easy way or the hard way.

She deposited a tablet in my lap.

—Don't talk, just watch.

It was the footage from the previous evening. Me at the kitchenette bench, drinking beer after beer, slumped on the bench, scrolling desultorily through my phone. Eventually I stumbled to the bathroom, Porcini nipping at my heels, and through the bathroom door I'd forgotten to lock. I knew what was coming next, but I watched it to the end. Porcini was sitting in the corner of the room, stock still, looking at me with the whole world watching. There I was, on all fours in the shower. When the vomiting began Porcini whined, trotted over to lick my face, and I screeched *no*, an awful guttural sound.

—There's a way for us to spin this, Jan said. What I'm saying is you have *options.*

She produced papers. I gave the documents a cursory read: transfers of ownership, non-disclosure agreements, money.

—What you do in the privacy of your own home is your business. *In theory*. But the optics are, and I can't put this forcefully enough, not good.

Jan helped me pack a bag, called me a cab to the airport. Porcini was asleep on his mat the whole time, didn't even wake when I stroked his belly to say goodbye. It was probably for the best. From the beginning, Jan had never trusted me. I was lazy, passive, ill-equipped to deal with life in the public eye. They drafted a press release explaining my absence, the usual excuses: a nervous breakdown, substance addiction. It was the end, for me and for *A Dog's Life*, as it turned out. In the following months, I received hate mail and death threats from dog lovers the world over; I was doxxed, glitterbombed, spat on.

The hush money was enough to buy this unit in West Footscray. When I can't sleep, I skulk through Porcini's Instagram. I've been diligently scrubbed from his feed; it's as if I never existed. I scroll until my thumbs ache, until I come across the photograph of Kaitlin's face hovering reverentially above Porcini's upturned snout. It's one of my best: perfectly composed, painterly even, their faces bathed in klieg light, a bottle of Suntory placed on the countertop behind them.

On Tightarse Tuesday I go to see *A Dog's Life* at the Sun Theatre in Yarraville. The film ends with a scene of Adam Driver sitting in a fleabag Melbourne apartment. His laptop is open on the grimy coffee table and he's watching the first video I uploaded to YouTube: *Rescue Dog Cooks a Banquet*. The camera pans in on his face, unmistakably middle-aged. Adam famously put on twenty kilograms for the role; he ate nothing but KFC for three months. Before the screen fades to black the frame tightens, until it's just Adam's eyes, smouldering with an intensity I could never muster in real life. In the background the sound of eggs sizzling on a skillet, Porcini barking, and my voice, thin and bright like an arrow, exclaiming: What is happening?

Sitting there in the darkened cinema, I imagine him, my dog, waking in the dark, as he often used to, sniffing for my scent, calling out for me, a summons I can never answer.

Qobad

Behrouz Boochani

Translated by Amir Ahmadi Arian

He crested the hill and sat on a rock, put down his Russian rifle and unhooked his bullet belt. He placed it on a dry camelthorn bush and lit a cigarette, taking deep drags as he stared at his weapon. Six months had passed since he'd last shot that gun, and that was to scare away the boars rolling around the wheatfield. He had no reason to carry that heavy thing everywhere, but over the years it had become a habit he could no longer shed. He would pick it up absent-mindedly every time he left the village, the same way he picked up his water canteen, and carried the gun like his balance depended on it, though he had vowed never to use it to kill a human being again.

No one knew about this pledge. Twenty years had passed since the last killing. Since then, he had gone to no one's house in the middle of the night to put a bullet in their heads. But the people in the village seemed to have failed to notice that. They still knew him as 'The Great Qobad', and still wove legends and stories about him and his gun.

From where he was sitting, the village resembled a stack of delicately placed matchboxes, with clay-and-straw roofs and granite walls. The autumn was drawing to an end. The first rain came down late this year, and now the village was preparing for the first snow. From his seat, Qobad could see the farmers bringing piles of wood down from the grey mountains on the backs of their donkeys and mules, hoarding them near the hedges of their yards. This was their last opportunity to get ready for winter, before the first snow laid siege to the village and entrapped the villagers for a few long months.

Qobad extinguished his cigarette, wrapped the bullet belt back around his waist, threw his gun on his shoulder and descended the hill. He walked across its brown, barren skirts and ran into a young shepherd. The man waved in response to his greetings, then picked up a rock and threw it at the wild goats grazing near his herd. Qobad got to the bridge that functioned as the village gate. An old woman with a heavy bag on her back walked past him. They exchanged a 'good afternoon,' then Qobad turned into the alley where, years ago, he had killed her cousin. This family feud was now old enough that he could see the dead man's family without feeling terrible.

A group of kids were riding sticks, pretending to be on horseback. One of them screamed 'Qobad!' and they scattered like a flock of geese noticing a fox. He always liked kids. If they stuck around and got close, he would kiss their heads and put some raisins in their pockets and chat with them. But that didn't change the way most children regarded him. They often fled as soon as they saw him.

He turned onto an alley that connected with the village's only street. A group of women sat on the steps of a house, chatting. When he emerged, they retreated inside and closed the door. He had to pause in the middle of the alley to wait for a herd of hungry goats to sprint across into a corral. The shepherd was holding open the gate, watching Qobad with worried eyes. The birds shrieked and the cattle bellowed. The village was fraught with sounds portending the arrival of winter.

Then he noticed people gathering at the mouth of the alley. Doors were thrown open and people ran out towards the street. A crowd came from behind and engulfed him. Some ignored him, others threw him a furtive greeting and headed to the street. He followed them to the village main square. On the surrounding rooftops women were standing, holding small children. This kind of gathering was rare, and occurred only when someone was killed or two families engaged in a bloody fight over water or land.

As he approached, a few people came forwards to welcome him. Among them he spotted his nephew, Rasoul. He looked exhausted and his ears were red. Spittle had dried on his lips.

'Uncle Qobad,' he said. 'God knows I wanted to load the gun you gave my father, but my mother didn't let me. She said we had to wait for you.'

Qobad didn't answer. He approached the crowd. People on his left and right called his name. He ignored them. He was headed for the huddle of the elders, but before he could get to them the villagers had surrounded him. They all spoke at the same time and he understood none of them, but he could read in their eyes all he needed to know. They wanted from him what they always wanted. The villagers regarded him as a boulder, using his shade in hot summers and hiding behind him to wait out the blizzards. He never wanted to play this role, but life had put him here, as if he was predestined for it.

An old man shuffled towards the circle. The crowd opened up to show respect. He came through, his cane beating against the stone, and stood face to face with Qobad.

'Qahraman was here,' the old man said, pausing to let the news sink in. 'Qahraman and his men were here last night.'

Qahraman was a name that made everyone tremble in fear. He was a vile, violent man, his brutality the stuff of legend in the area. Everybody in the mountains was convinced that nothing could stop Qahraman, that he transcended laws and rules. He was heartless enough, the stories had it, to steal babies from their swaddles or shoot at the belly of a pregnant woman. Every time he bore down on a village he left burnt, ashen land in his wake. He had been encircled by the guards many times, and in every case he slithered out of the siege like a snake. There were numerous tales about him, and in every one of them he was a winner. Last night he was there, in the village that had Qobad as its protector, the man whom everybody feared and trusted. Because of Qobad, no one thought Qahraman would ever dare to touch this corner of the mountains.

'They were twelve horsemen,' the old man continued. 'They threatened bloodshed.'

A cold snowflake landed on Qobad's aquiline nose. He looked up at the creamy sky, the flurry of snow that fell but mostly melted before reaching the earth, except for the larger flakes that powered through and landed on the wrinkled, leathery skin of the men around him.

'Qahraman had come to claim Chiasooz.'

Chiasooz. The word is soaked in old blood. When Qobad was a child, several villages were fighting over the Chiasooz plain. When he was six, in that final attack that defeated his village and made his people flee to the mountains, he was left behind. All of a sudden he found himself alone, wandering around barefoot, crying and calling for his mother. On the hilltop the galloping horses were kicking up dust, and from the dust emerged the towering silhouettes of gunmen as they attacked his village. This image was etched indelibly in his mind, and it surfaced every time he sensed a threat to his village. Qobad had survived. His father, midway through his escape, noticed that his son was not with them. He had returned to the village and snatched Qobad away just before the gunmen arrived.

The fight over Chiasooz went on for a long time, and white flags were raised only when the war became unfeasible for all sides. The plain was divided among the villages. Peace had ruled over the mountains ever since, until now, with Qahraman emerging to tell them that he was planning to end it.

'Qahraman insulted you,' the old man said, holding a red cloth in his hands. 'He threw this scarf, and told us to hang it from the wall of your house.'

Qobad fastened his pitch-black eyes to the ground. He scratched his thick beard, then his cheeks, which were now red with rage. He had tried for twenty years to build a new reputation. He didn't want to be known as the mountain rebel. His presence still inspired fear, but many had accepted his new character. These days he regarded himself as a farmer, a man like others who spent their lives working on the land. Twenty years had passed, and now only old people had firsthand memories of his killing spree and his violence. He was *this* close to a new life.

But was he truly upset? Deep inside, he knew that he wasn't. Despite all his efforts, a stronger impulse, albeit dormant, still lurked inside him. Rebellion was in his flesh and blood, woven into the fabric of who he was. But no, he thought. He would have to contain himself.

'It is snowing tonight,' he yelled assertively.

The crowd hummed.

'Don't you see? It is snowing tonight.'

Quizzical looks were cast at him from all directions. Bodies fidgeted and jolted. They heard fear in his scream, and his fear made them afraid. They watched his large bulk lumber away from them, heading towards home.

The crowd stirred. The voices rose. The youths encircled the old man who had delivered the news to Qobad. It was hard to believe that Qobad, 'The Great Qobad', had his head down like a scared dog and was walking away.

Qobad took twenty steps, then bent over, as if under the weight of the looks from the villagers. He took off one of his shoes and shook it to remove a pebble. Then he put it back on, tightened his belt, took a few more steps, swivelled and stared at the crowd. He uttered no words and he didn't have to. In his silent way, he was communicating to them that he would no longer protect them. He kept staring defiantly. His dark gaze made the crowd scatter. The last person standing was the old man, leaning against his cane, shaking his head and whispering under his breath. Then he shuffled across the street and entered the coffee house.

The nephew, Rasoul, standing under the shed in front of a house, watched Qobad disappear around the corner. He then followed the old man inside the coffee house and crept into a corner by the fire. About fifty other men had gathered around the burning wood, sitting on chairs and tree trunks. Rasoul watched the young worker run out of the store to fetch large pieces of wood, shove them into the fire and settle a kettle on the burgeoning flames. The sharp smell of wet wood and cigarette smoke filled the air.

Everybody was talking disparagingly of Qobad. *He is not the man he used to be*, they said. *He sounded ridiculous.* Rasoul listened in silence, feeling humiliated and paralysed, as if he were watching them bury someone he loved and admired.

The debate was soon polarised along a generational divide. The youth were up in arms, screaming that they didn't need Qobad, that they could take care of Qahraman on their own. The old man sucked his teeth and warned them against hasty decisions, but they ignored him, drowned him out, even screamed at him, blood boiling in their veins.

'This is not who we are. We won't sit back and watch someone come from five villages away to claim our land.'

'Forget about the old Qobad. He hasn't killed an ant in twenty years. He avoids blood at any cost.'

'You talk like you don't know Qobad. The man has killed at least twenty people.'

'That was the old times. Now he's like a dove.'

'You're wrong. He is called "The Great Qobad" for a reason.'

'All the greatness he has, he owes it to this land. If we lose it, nothing about him or us will be great anymore.'

'You know how many people will die if we go to war with Qahraman? Leave it to Qobad. He'll figure out a way.'

'You folks seem to forget that we are not the only people with claim to Chiasooz. It belongs to other villages too. Even if we give up, those folks won't let Qahraman take it.'

'But Qahraman doesn't care about other villages. He is happy to share it with them. He is just after us because he wants to beat Qobad.'

'This is not about a piece of land. This is about our dignity.'

'At the end of the day, we have no warrior who's anything like Qobad.'

'What should we do, old man?'

'Yes, uncle, please tell us what we should do, now that Qobad has hung us out to dry?'

The air was stuffy with the vapour out of the kettle and smoke and human breath, but at least it was warm. Outside, a thick layer of grey, loaded clouds choked the sky. Rasoul stayed silent but didn't miss a word. As it grew colder, men dragged their chairs and tree stumps closer to the fire.

'It looks like Qobad doesn't want us to go to war against Qahraman,' the old man said.

'But what will people think? How will other villages look at us?'

'Qobad will find a way to solve this issue without bloodshed. We need to give him time.'

'He doesn't seem to care.'

'Shut your mouth!' cried Rasoul from his corner, finally finding his voice. 'If it weren't for Qobad, Qahraman would have razed this village to the ground a hundred times by now.'

'Qobad is a coward,' said a fat young man, sitting far from the crowd.

All heads turned to him. He had said what was on everyone's mind but no one had dared to articulate.

Rasoul lunged at him and threw him on the heap of wood behind the fire. The two men grappled and wrestled each other to the ground and fought among the legs of the others. The crowd separated them. Rasoul rose, his nose bloody, his clothes covered with the sawdust from the floor. He left the coffee house, cursing the village and its people, and headed towards Qobad's house.

The street was empty. A scattering of small, feeble snowflakes whirled in the air. He kept his head up and pinched his nose to staunch the blood, thinking of the stories he grew up hearing about his uncle. In the space of a single evening, his image of Qobad had been shattered. All the honour and glory he had brought to his family name had vanished, and now they were associated with this pathetic man who curled up in a corner as soon as he faced danger. Rasoul was incensed. If Qobad shirked that fight it would be a blow to the reputation of their entire family.

He entered into Qobad's house without knocking. This was a disrespectful thing to do, but he couldn't care less. Inside the house, in a large shadowy room, his aunt was sitting by the fire, stitching an old blanket. She glanced at Rasoul's bloodshot eyes and returned to sewing without uttering a word.

This was nothing new to Bati. Since she was eighteen, her life had been all about Qobad and other men fighting and shooting at each other. Her rhythm of sewing accelerated with Rasoul's arrival. He grabbed the metal prod and turned the fire over, then sat down and stared at the flames. The room had a fretful air as if it awaited terrible news.

'Where is Uncle Qobad?' Rasoul asked.

'What happened to your nose?'

'I had a fight over him.'

'Since when do people here fight over Qobad?'

'Word has gotten around that he is scared of Qahraman. People are insulting our family.'

Bati stopped sewing.

'People love to gossip.'

'But what they say—'

Something in the woman's gaze silenced Rasoul. They sat together quietly, watching the flames. She was thinking of all the days Qobad spent away from home, all those nights of loneliness, raising their children with no help, no money and, hardest of all, the cruel snark people kept hurled her, the pitying tone when they talked to her children, the spiteful way of expressing concern that the kids were growing up fatherless.

Qobad left the village again, but this time no one thought he would disappear for so long. Many were confident that he was dead, fallen victim to hungry bears or murdered in a fight. A rumour began to circulate that he had crossed the border and started a new family on the other side. A story came from a hunter who claimed to have seen him, but as soon as he called his name Qobad jumped up and climbed the hill like a wild goat and disappeared. They called him 'The Coward Qobad', added bitterness seeping in with the winter months and Qahraman's new reign. His wife heard it all, and although she believed none of it, every story was a stab in her heart.

Then, late in the spring, Qobad suddenly showed up in the village again. Nothing in his appearance gave any clue as to where he had been or what he had endured. The bones in his face were prominent and his frame erect, just as it had been in his younger days, as if all along he had been a ghost wandering around, waiting for the right moment to materialise. In his typically cold demeanour, he walked home through the transfixed crowd. No one dared to ask him where he had been. How horrible were the long years of his absence, his wife was now thinking with her nephew at her side, all the years she fought to keep their children alive. Bati was no longer young. She couldn't deal with another disappearance.

There was a noise outside. Qobad had arrived at the threshold of his home. His shoes were soaked. He eyed Rasoul and sat down next to his wife.

'I am so hungry,' he said, like a child.

The woman fetched a large bowl of soup and a piece of bread from the kitchen. Rasoul was gone when she came back. He hadn't exchanged a word with his uncle. Qobad broke the bread into the soup and ate it all, then lay down and closed his eyes.

Coldness woke him up. He rubbed his eyes. The fire was dying. He turned over the coals and dropped in a piece of wood. Yellow light stirred on the walls. He pulled on his wool socks and threw a piece of bread and cheese into his rucksack. From the shack in the yard he grabbed his gun and left. It was time.

He climbed the hill behind the village. From the top, the village looked like a cave whose ceiling was lit up by fireflies. On the other side of the hill, he no longer heard the dogs barking. An intense, complete silence reigned over the valley, a silence so profound it was as if it had never been disturbed by a human presence.

He did what he had always done—leaving the village quietly, no hesitation in his legs, carrying the same rucksack, his old bullet belt and the gun he had owned for decades. Now he was at the bottom of the valley, walking down the path where he had ridden his horse countless times as a child. As he climbed over the last rock he was overwhelmed with the sense of ending. No more hiding. No more running away.

He entered the territory of the next village. Not that anything was unfamiliar. From the entire region he had countless memories, years of war and peace, many weddings and funerals. Lights flickered all across the mountainside at regular distances, like a gold chain hung unevenly around a neck.

He found a cave and crept into it. He put up his cold, wet feet and leaned against its wall. He rolled a cigarette and looked down at the village from above. Now here he was, on the hill at whose feet lay the village where Qahraman was sleeping in its tallest and sturdiest house, likely next to a woman forced to spend the night with him.

Qobad had become like a ghost, like the old Qobad, with dead, black eyes, the invisible assassin whom the strongest ramparts could not hold at bay. Now he had to climb down the hill, step over the puddles and into soft mud, watching his shadow flickering on the village walls as he approached his prey. If anyone heard him, he would take them out with a blow to the temple. Getting to Qahraman's house, he would crouch and move soundlessly along the wall and climb it at its darkest spot, in the midpoint between the big lights, one for the stable and the other for the house. He would rip the back door curtain and snake inside, silently creeping through the rooms to get to Qahraman.

He was not the type who shoots as soon as they get a chance. His fingers would beg to pull the trigger, but he would resist. This was part of his ritual, his private ceremony of bloodshed. He might even drag Qahraman out of the bed, make him raise his hands and put the bullet in his stomach from close range. He considered humiliating Qahraman some more. He would be the god in that room after all, for he would be the one with his finger on the trigger, the one that the gun would obey.

But he wanted to keep it simple this time. He would put a bullet in his stomach, then one in his head for good measure, then run back and climb the wall and disappear into the dark. Qobad would cross through the village and sprint alongside the graveyard, his steps fast and long, and then wade through the snow to get to the mountains. Behind him there would rise a commotion, the screams of the gunmen running everywhere, then the barrage of gunshots travelling toward him.

Tamanu

Josephine Rowe

The saint is nameless when she comes to Orrin Bird. By horse float, of all means. Though he cannot say what other mode of transport might have been more appropriate, given circumstances. She could hardly have come by rail, accompanied or otherwise. He supposes she might have come by hearse. Though hearses are scarce enough out here, and to receive a casket, a box of any kind from such a vehicle, would have brought attention, prying in the guise of condolences. In fact, condolences are not unwarranted—his old friend, Kaspar Isaksen, is gone, has finally drunk himself to death, and left Orrin custodian to a saint.

Bequest is how she is detailed, by Isaksen's solicitor, in the letter that preceded her arrival. The saint had been nameless, too, when she came to Kaspar himself. Removed from whatever place she had been kept and cared for, for however long, and where she was presumably entreated with a name, one lost now. How had she come to Kaspar, on that speck of phosphate in the Central Pacific? Likely no respectable avenue.

Canonisation unverified, the letter notes. Then goes on to submit that an incorruptible body, however, delivered of all evidence of earthly violences and earthly sufferings, is typically considered grounds enough for beatification. Beatification, at the least.

Orrin—not devout, or not in a Catholic sense—is conflicted about the nature of this legacy. He has no notion of how to care for a saint. Even a small one. Does not even believe. Not in any one God, attended by angels and casting His divine judgement down from On High. If he has gods, they are many, and they themselves tend—are the kind who get their hands dirty and wet, who are the Dirt and the Wet. And yes, the Dry. Terrible Dry, who no doubt has no comprehension nor will towards terror. Just Is. As are the gods Salt and Reef and Ant Mound. The birds who tell him whether he is or isn't home.

Still. Catholic or not. You don't turn away a saint.

He wears his best clothes to receive her, feeling foolish. An olive-green coat that belonged to his father, too heavy for the Kimberley heat at any time of year. The horse float is fine, as horse floats go. It survives the journey—his house some way from town, and the road neither well made nor well travelled. Two men unhitch the float from their truck and leave it freighted. They speak to one another in a northern language. To Orrin, they speak very little. He signs a paper and they leave him with the float.

The interior of the float smells only faintly of the beasts it was intended for. More strongly, to him, it smells of an island church. A scent he's not known for a quarter century, since he left that looted rock for home.

Orrin Bird knows wood. He knows hulls and decks, and the frames of houses. Machines, also, both heavy and light. But mostly he knows wood. The box—coffin-like, after all—is built of canoe timber, tamanu. He recognises it as his own craft. Kaspar had asked for a box, providing exact specifications, twenty-five or more years ago. Said it was for blankets. Tamanu still grew abundant on the island's central plateau then, had not yet been ploughed down in ceaseless gouging for phosphate.

At sixty-five, the rigging of his back is still dependable. When he carries the box into the shade of the house, it seems to weigh less than when first fashioned. Lighter than the planks he'd salvaged and cut for it.

How small is she, inside, and how old? How long did she have in warm, living years? (The letter suggests eleven.) And after? In the dormant, closed-in years? The style of her garments supposedly dates to the early eighteenth century, to Europe, but the solicitor's letter allows that they might have been chosen to give the appearance of antiquity. Or, conversely, they might have been serially replaced, updated over time, in accordance with changing fashions or conventions. The garments are painstakingly, tediously described. So she is eleven, or she is two hundred and fifty. Or older still, or somewhere between. He does not care to open the box and appraise the garments for himself, to reckon on their authenticity.

The girl in her box—in the box he built for her, unwitting—warrants a name. Orrin can think only of his mother. His mother was a hard woman. Poured boiling water on the dogs' feed so that they wouldn't wolf it. Her son's, too. But she was a read woman. Countless thick books by Russians, stacked high as the bureau when she was ordered bed rest—he remembers—for the flutter of a sister. The sister did not last. Still, a name was kept for her. (Was his mother hard, before this? Not known.)

He names the saint for his sister, with no sense of trespass.

He is not versed in the ways of saints. Never having cared for anything but machines and plants and dogs. Orrin's dogs need only fuel and coaxing words. Dampier dogs, of no discernible breeding. He lets them eat at whatever speeds please them.

First dog, White, returns from wherever she's been, red Pindan dust socking her legs, having stained them that way. Forever, it seems. Again and again, he has sent White dog into the surf, after sticks, to bathe her. Each time, she re-emerges looking just the same, but happier.

Second dog, Blue, lags behind in a sore-footed dance, paws stuck full of bindis. Blue dog always finds the bindis. Orrin unsticks them; this is the game.

Let inside the house, the dogs settle immediately in front of the box, and that, to him, is proof enough. He trusts his dogs. He trusts what his dogs trust, bindi patches excepted.

With the saint seen to, overseen, he comes down to the business of missing his friend.

O f course she has a name, one she was given at birth. And then lived inside, almost long enough to get used to it. But that much, the name at least, she is keeping for herself. There are people, still alive, still referring to her by this name. And she is not, has never been a saint. That hardly needs saying. She is a kid in a box tens of thousands of miles from where she died, with no way back to that place. A kid in a box whose body—Gott fuck them—is still somehow of interest to men. When she died, she was already tired of her body being of interest to men. She was fourteen and slight for her age, but that didn't stop them. Did not even slow them down. You'd think death would have taken care of that.

She never learned to read but could swear in four languages. Five, now. No accounting for it, the way certain

46

things just keep on, banking up. An art to it. An ear. Picking up every shiny dangerous thing dropped from the mouths of canal workers, sailors, in the backstreets of her first city. An ever-expanding arsenal of savage little implements she could conceal on her small person, test the keenness of now and again. Especially on North Americans, milk-soft, with their yellow gases for killing mosquitoes, their pockets full of chewing gum and scraps for cooing strays.

She has always been fond of dogs, and dogs of her. She prefers dogs to people. If she has ever been saint to anyone or anything, it was to one mutt. Who knew what he knew, that dog. Only that when he smelled smoke he went crazy. Running around whimpering with nowhere to go. She protected him from the everyday demon of smoke. He was tiny and hurt and could not return the favour. That was all right. He let her be a kid with a dog. She rubbed the bare, pink patches on his haunches and tail, soft as she could.

For the record, it was a very popular name, in her grandmother's time, when her grandmother was a girl. In fact, it was her grandmother's name—there you have it. (Her sister has a daughter, now, and the daughter has her name. It is spoken aloud every day, many times.)

In her first city, girls her age and younger grew accustomed to the rasp of fresh stubble. Or no, not accustomed to, never really accustomed to—familiar with. Men still shaved, wanted to look respectable to fuck a child. Some girls had tricks to make themselves less girl, less appealing. Wearing their brothers' clothes, for instance. Letting their hair hang in rank snakes or hacking it away altogether. Walking like maybe they had something you didn't want to catch. Acting wild, plain crazy.

She herself was famous at crazy, convincing, bugging her eyes and twitching her limbs and swearing in her several bad languages at imaginary devils whenever a stranger approached. She might have been an actress, might have got around the world that way.

But it happened to her anyhow.

Her sister once told her that every woman who dies like that has already dreamed her death.

And girls?

Girls too. The smart ones.

She was smart. Smarter than most. Had she dreamed her death, then, or one like it? She must have. Stories of that kind went around all the time.

For a time, it had looked like she might yet survive it.

But after it happened. After that happened. Well, after that happens, some said, almost better to die sweet than to live and grow bitter. They'd seen women grow bitter after living through a thing like that, and no, it was not a pretty sight. It bled your heart. A waste of womanhood, a sinful waste. Better to die sweet, and stay that way.

Death had not sweetened her. It had only enraged her. In death, she grew ever more enraged. The things they'd costumed her in. A joke. A joke and a lie—never in life had she worn anything so elaborately suffocating. Or hideous. Or impractical. If she had been caught going around alive in this trashy finery, someone would have slapped her. Right down from off her high horse. And she hadn't gone into the vault that way, either. No one had seen the cause for that kind of extravagance. Of course they hadn't.

Incorruptible. Who'd have guessed. (No one, that's who.)

That her body did not corrupt accordingly was not miraculous. It was perverse. That her flesh did not retain any trace of violence was a betrayal. It was absolution—she knew about absolution, what and whom it was really for—and if it had been up to her, she would not have given it. If it had been up to her, she would have rained fire and much worse upon that man and all men like him. Called all the ants down from the anthills. Made it slow. If it had been up to her.

It was a curse in some places, some parts of the world: May the earth not eat you.

In older—better—stories, no one is forgiven, and the girl escapes by becoming a tree. A laurel, or a poplar. Or a star. Even a stone—she could settle for being stone. People once believed that stones could grow, and why not? Limestone was just life heaped up on life heaped up on life and then pressed down hard over millennia. And after all that, people come along and mine it to the surface and grind it to powder and sprinkle it around again in order to call forth more life.

It's a long process. But if you could learn to think in mountaintime, it might come to seem very simple. But people are mostly stupid, very sentimental, very attached to their human time. And even mountains can be annihilated, flattened in a matter of puny human years, their insides quarried away for this or for that so in the end they collapse like an old, crushed fedora. In the end, it's best not to get too attached, to dogs or mountains, to anything at all.

Why not die of yellow fever, like everyone else? Then at least she might have found some peace.

There might still be time to become a tree. If offered a choice, she would prefer tree. Her tree-self would be the kind with poisonous spines that only certain birds and animals could negotiate, and whose fruits appeal only to bats. Needless to mention the armies of fierce stinging ants that would shelter in her limbs and be under her dominion.

K aspar Isaksen had been dispatched to the Micronesian island to observe its lazaret: a mile-long stretch of coastline designated for the more infectious cases of Hansen's disease. A byproduct of the phosphate industry, as he saw it, and corollary of any industry that rested upon indentured labour. He had been sent out by a Norwegian university on a three-month appointment, a term he had overstayed by several years. Before this minor mutiny, he had observed at Palo Seco, the Dry Stick Colony, in the Canal Zone. Still held as keepsakes the loose brass and aluminium tokens that were the currency of that place. He had a wife and a son who had followed him to Panama—and lived very comfortably as Zonians, it must be said—but who would no longer follow and had since returned to Oslo. The son grown, now, in any case. The wife grown increasingly ornery, and somewhat narrow in her allowances.

The Norwegian was a great admirer of Hansen. He still referred to the malady as Hansen's disease, though it was no longer called by that name. He still referred to the island as Pleasant. Its remoteness made conditions for study exceptionally favourable.

Could a lazaret be made cheerful? Might the isolated come to feel less isolated, even content, within its confines? Kaspar—

who had been accorded no official title or duty by the Administration but who nevertheless believed the residents of the colony lay under his Protection—aided in the scheduling of brass bands and picture shows and itsibweb matches, a game whose ball was contrived from a rock wound around and around with pandanus leaves. There was rarely a bloodless match. He distributed reading material that trickled in second-hand from well-wishers in Australia and New Zealand. Conversations with unafflicted friends and relations were permitted at distances of sixteen feet. He learned much from the leeside.

Orrin had first come to the island to work on equipment that made other, distant men rich, other land rich, and the land he stood on poor, snaggled, martian. Then he worked for Kaspar, doing far less, and less harm. Simple carpentry with simple tools, sorting donations for the colony.

Kaspar brewed a tea that had the likeness of pale-green oil, very bitter, whose effect was soporific. Some cautioned against the invitation to drink, warned that the stuff would suppress a man's spirit, and leave him susceptible to the biddings of the Norwegian. Orrin half believed them. And he drank anyway. He is unsure whether his will was corrupted during that time. They never shared a bed through a full night. Waking alone, he rarely felt shame.

Kaspar had accumulated the names of all the birds on the island, in Nauruan and in English, and would offer these upon sight or sound. Thus, Orrin Bird received the names of all the birds. But their calls kept him awake in the darkness, niggled him. He'd lie there, alert and seething. Once or twice he opened a window and threw something. If he'd had a gun. Yes, he would have. Shot the bloody things down to earth. (He'd knocked once, in the riotous dawn dark, on Kaspar's door, and asked to borrow his rifle. Kaspar knew better than to let him, sent him away placated with some concoction for sleep.)

The Norwegian assented to eating fish from the sea but saw no reason in causing profitless harm to any creature. During crab time, when the lowlands were a sideways-shifting carpet of crustaceans, the older man erected temporary plank walkways so as not to crush them underfoot. He adopted the local sport of luring and taming frigates. The purring clicks and croaks of frigates were a soothing timpani to Kaspar, to most others. Not to Orrin.

In the Kimberley, it's never been that way. Here, where he can barely distinguish one bird from the next, they've always sounded sweet to him. Even the shrillest of them. Even when they roust him from sleep. They'll just as likely soothe him back.

Maybe that's how you know where home is. The birds don't chivvy you so much.

Night; the saint in the kitchen. The dogs, for once, do not scratch at his door to get into his bed. Of course he dreams her. And when she appears, it is not in the burden of deep velvet and Alençon lace, nor the rich silks as inventoried in the letter. Nor the ridi, nor any other exotic flourish.

The saint, the girl, Irina, is dressed in ordinary linen, sweat- and salt-stiff, dark circles under her eyes already. Born tired. She is brusque and without patience for fools, nor for penitents. Pushes her long dark hair from her face with a fury that is familiar to him. She pours forth from a ragbag of languages, of which he understands only a little, a few intermittent words, mostly the swearing. She curses precociously. She curses blue murder. Profanities suited to sailors and miners, blasphemy inflected by the German Gott, the French putain. She goes barefoot at the height of the day, over the scorching claypans and with the baking red dirt swilling up to her ankles. Goes slowly and unflinching, as no stranger to this place, to this dust, ever could.

Apart from this inviolability, he suspects that she is not miraculous, that she is of no greater faith or sanctity than he. He does not say so.

On waking, he has no desire either to confirm this vision or to relinquish it. No desire to open the tamanu box and compare the image to the earthly, incorruptible stuff. He desires, in fact, not to. Fears she will not return.

Among his other, more practical fears: that white ants will devour the box. Their pillars rise up sentinel from the surrounding scrub, advancing in stature and girth by the year. He keeps the habit of measuring, with tape and logbook. Refers to them by character, or cardinal, or by simple reference points. Mammoth: nearest to water tank. Goliath: seaward. David: east of Goliath. He places his ear to their pocked hulls, fancies he can hear their industry.

Certain times—at the brief, colourless edges of the day— their ghostly forms put him in mind of the crags and pinnacles of fossilised coral, the chewed-out core of the eviscerated island, gouged up and hauled away to be processed for fertiliser. Though whatever the hour, and whether lit by sun or moon, those exhausted monoliths resembled tombstones. Unlike the ant homes, they had no resonance, no language, told of no cloistered animation within. Only of depletion—a boneyard that expanded steadily, by the year. Markers to yet another, more enduring affliction come to bear upon the island.

The work that had taken him there was instrumental to this decimation. The island, encircled by reef, had no harbour. The cantilever was three years' construction. At last, its gargantuan insectile arms swung over the barricade of coral and then back out to the freighters anchored offshore, bearing crushed phosphate at a thousand tons an hour.

Yes, it was impressive to witness, a feat of engineering. And yes, the dust powdered everything. Orrin wheezed in it. He'd come to this trade because his shallow lungs were no good for diving. Nor were they good for any war.

His father had pearled, and fought, and sailed back from the Western Front to pearl again. Eventually, the sea just kept hold of him. Something Orrin remembers of his father: that he would not speak of the Front but during thunderstorms was given to recall the great cannonade of Krakatoa—he himself had heard it, from the schoolyard at Fremantle Boys'—and the incomparable sunsets that came after. The persistent ring around the sun, and how folk then spoke of the End. But it wasn't the End. So, there you have it: sometimes it looks like the End, but it isn't.

It was the End somewhere, put in Orrin's mother, from behind her book. For a great lot of folk, that was the End. Then she dipped her head back into Dostoyevsky's Russia.

Kaspar once told Orrin that he had the air of a man brought up amongst sisters. This was not intended as insult; Orrin did not take it as insult. Though he had no sisters, only the enduring shadow of one.

It's true that her eyes might open on occasion. Or appear to open, to whoever might be observing. This is a common enough phenomenon. One distinguished with a Latin name, and in accordance with quantifiable exterior factors such as ambient temperature and humidity: when they brought her to the Kimberley, into the Dry, her eyelids shrank. Simple. In the Kimberley, her eyes are open more than half the year.

But in short, it makes no difference.

To speak of consciousness: complicated. What does she know, from this near remove? More and less. Her awareness is disengaged from human senses, is beyond human senses, but only so far. Not as far as could be hoped. Her little world.

Evening, when the house is thrown open to the westerly, and some skerrick of it steals in through the slats of tamanu, rustles the layers enveloping her within the box, it can't exactly be said that she feels the breeze cool on her skin. Only a recognition that there is breeze, that it comes from the west, that such a breeze would feel cool upon the skin. An awareness that the man, Orrin Bird, feels the breeze as cooling to his skin; that the dogs pant their relief into it, exchanging it for their hot yawns. It can be said that this is enjoyable, that satisfaction of a kind is still available to her. The man, Orrin, inclining his grey-ginger head, spreading his hands as if in praise, reaching into the current of air as if into a stream of water. She cannot know what her sister is doing. Sometimes, she hears her name.

Hears? To put it differently:

Sometimes, there is her name.

Her sister told of at least one woman who'd tried to fake her way into the leper colony, back in the Canal Zone. Life didn't cost anything there. And it was good enough for the Americans.

At Palo Seco, her sister prepared meals and medicines, crushing ripe seeds into the almost useless chaulmoogra oil. She swam in the lepers' sea, where others would never dare, for fear that the bacteria would wash down and infect them, the Clean.

The Norwegian watched her swim, and asked why she was not afraid. She had never been afraid, but even in her grief—proud idiot—she had to brag. She swiped the water from her limbs with the firm blade of her hand and answered: My sister is incorruptible.

And that did it. The Norwegian was all packed up for Oceania. But he asked to visit the girl saint.

Of course, and he was shown to where they had her laid out in that monstrous costume.

I see, he said. My word.

There was still the tedious matter of veneration, obtaining official recognition from the Church. The requisite petitioning, locally and abroad, miracles to be recorded and attested to, relics to be examined. Bureaucracies that ran far beyond the family's means and station.

Yes, of course he could assist. Use his standing and considerable et cetera et cetera, advance proceedings. His wife's brother, friend to a bishop, as it happened.

He was packed and ready, but he quietly made arrangements for more effects.

There are relics, you could call them that. They are objects of absolutely no use or importance to her: a comb, a holy book, some tacky beads and ornaments.

Other earthly things, still with her, more valuable:

The crackle and slow spill of honeycomb, snatched cool from storage, bitten into on a hot morning.

The tug of her sister's fingers combing her hair with a bright-smelling balm, impatient but not ungentle.

Her own fingers sifting the shore, slivers of coral and ossified wood slipping through.

The ocean carrying her on its breath.

When Orrin returned to Western Australia from Micronesia, the Tasmanian tiger was newly extinct, and his mother had lost the words for simple things. Handed a teacup, she'd call it a chaucer. You had to laugh, except when you couldn't. In his mind, these losses were linked, threads of a greater diminishing.

And then another war. He was too old by then for his bad lungs to matter. Japan bombed Darwin in the summer of '42, and strafed Broome two weeks later. Roebuck Bay skeined with burning oil, and flying boats blazing down into it, laden with Dutch refugees bound for sanctuary.

Letters arrived from the Manawatu; Kaspar had removed himself to New Zealand, to whatever distant family he had there, to wait out the worst of it. Nauru had been subject to several raids, by air and by sea. Kaspar did not see its occupation. At last, he missed his homeland. His wife and his son. Still, it was the island he vowed a return to, whatever might be left of it, once the war closed down.

Orrin's mother died believing the war would last forever. Did that matter? No, it was all the same war anyway. Sometimes it looked like the End, but it wasn't.

(Hiroshima. Nagasaki. For a great lot of folk: yes.)

In the years that followed, Kaspar Isaksen went about the slow, methodical task of drinking himself to death. His letters came clogged with remorse for fates he'd not learned of until after the war. For instance how, during the occupation, his former charges had been rounded up from their cultivated strip of coast and loaded into small boats, and the boats towed out to sea, shelled and sunk. Thus leprosy was removed from the island. He had withdrawn his Protection, he scratched, in a script crouched by shame and by guilt, and his wards had suffered the greatest consequence.

Protection. Orrin initially reckoned the capitalisation a habitual Scandinavian slip by the inebriated Norwegian, nothing to do with divinity. Kaspar's correspondence made no other allusion to the saint, even then.

What could a lone man have done? would have been Orrin's reply, had he given one. Been drowned alongside, like the rest?

But he had not replied.

Now, understanding what was meant by Protection, he might simply have gestured towards Europe: teeming with saints, and still full of bomb craters.

The first box was formed of rough planks, birch. It carried her across the North Pacific, away from her isthmus.

She knew the lives of those birch, before they were planks.

For a tree, being a box is much the same as being a saint: your own life is over, but people are still bothering you, expecting you to help. She felt bad for the birch.

This box is built of boat wood. But placed half a day's walk from water. In any case, it isn't properly sealed; air gets in. What is she supposed to do out here?

Sometimes, he leaves the radio on.

Sometimes, there is her name.

If she had survived, she might still be alive. Middle-aged, now. Grown bitter, but perhaps loved for it, even so. Bitter has its merits, its sophistications. Bitter is a rite, a taste you can acquire.

People go to some trouble to acquire a taste for it. It's something. Sweet is nothing. Sweet is for children, for a child squatting on a stone floor with a stolen honeycomb. A minor art made of melting and dividing nectar from wax in her mouth, spitting out the hard globs to save for wax animals.

But then, she might not have been bitter at all. She might have been formidable, and worldly. She might have brought down fire and ants and worse, and then simply stepped away and left them to it. Made the same passage by choice, upright, in simple linen. Not as cargo. Might have come all this way out of wanderlust, because she felt like it, then planted her hands and feet in the red soil and grown here.

She might have passed by this man, his blue dog and his dirty white dog, and they would have regarded one another, briefly and without obligation, and wished well, and gone on.

Every few summers, cyclones come to thrash the region, and his house is spared. He does not believe the girl is a saint. He does not believe she is his sister. And yet, and yet.

For the seventeen years left to him, he dreams most nights of her small, furious face, and wakes now and then with the feeling of polished stones slipping cool through his fingers, a sound like rain or the wind that shows the pale undersides of leaves, stood at the edge of knowing something of magnitude. For seventeen years, he wakes with the feeling and lets the feeling dim, lets it go. Then he gets up, feeds the dogs, goes out into the dark to piss, tows the dinghy to the sea, puts the dinghy on the water, and waits. Says his sister's name aloud, sometimes, in greeting or parting, never entreats her for anything more.

He lives small amidst the ant mounds, constructs a greenhouse of salvaged windows and sheet plastic to cultivate seeds carried home in his pockets, many years before, varieties he suspects no longer grow on the island from which he gathered them. No noteworthy harm comes to him before his time, by which point it is not met as harm. The dogs, White and Blue, are long since. He passes on without will or testament. He makes no provision or instruction for the girl, the maybe-saint.

Around the house, the ant mounds grow in stature and girth. White ants do not eat the box. White ants do not care for tamanu. They devour instead: the stumps and joists, the posts and beams. The floor goes soft. The verandah gives way. The roof buckles in on itself. The ant mounds grow in stature, and in girth.

The greenhouse lasts longer than it should, until the plastic is brittled by the Dry, ribboned by the Wet. The plants wither and crisp. Rabbits and possums chew what's left down to the roots.

Now and then, an animal thumping through the ruin of what had once been a house, a bird preparing its home above a lintel. She is aware of the sea drawing closer.

The Station

Kathryn Gledhill-Tucker

Tali's morning commute to the radio station is always wet. It is a slow and careful walk. The bitumen street wears a layer of algal slime that makes her shoes glide. As Tali drags her legs through water, she dodges a school of small fish and their winged predators. She greets them sweetly, even if it adds a good half an hour to her trip each way.

Boordawan FM stands like a spite house between office buildings, hidden in the central business district. It's several storeys of brick, with large windows that look out over the city. Ellie walks briskly through the foyer, with the pleasure of introducing Jack to the station for the first time.

'Our lovely Tali secured this space with a government grant that helps to keep the lights on. Day to day, the ground floor is usually filled with artists and researchers, mostly doing cultural consulting work and planning some large-scale murals.' Ellie gestures to the far wall, which is plastered with a black-and-white illustration of the city, and the words *Make Noise Boorloo* painted in large block letters in the centre. 'The building belongs to the trust now, which is I-M-O one of the better uses of those mining royalties.'

'True, hey.' Jack was familiar enough with the companies whose names dominated the skyline outside and the effect they had on his hometown.

'It's basically a big, Blak radio station-slash-cooperative working space-slash-keeping place.'

'How long have you been working here?'

Jack had heard about these sovereign spaces cropping up around town, but this was his first time inside one. He was fresh out of high school. It felt warmer than he expected for an office, more worn and lived in.

'Almost six months.' Ellie's eyes shine through acrylic glasses and dark curls. 'Tali and I met each other at a rally. You can probably hear her broadcasting right now, but we can go say hi.' She points at speakers hanging from the ceiling.

The station lives under a flight path. From the window of the upstairs studio, around mid-morning, a family of karak scrawk their way towards a eucalyptus tree a hundred metres away. Their red tails, exposed from underneath, flash like five rogue embers darting the cloudless sky. Tali first noticed their daily voyage a week ago, when the air began to warm and the trees budded with flowers.

Settling into the second half of her morning set, Tali indulges in some favourites: Barkaa, RONA., a bit of Emily Wurramara. It's Tali's show, so she can play what she likes. She imagines the station's transmission tower taking these precious stories and turning them into vibrations in the air, amplifying them on their journey through the sky, transmitting them to people's homes, cars and ears. The air acting like both an envelope and an aeroplane.

As well as songs, Tali makes space to play a few new materials that have found a home in the archives. These pieces arrived at the station in stacks of cardboard boxes, donated by a local researcher's family. The collections hold hundreds of hours of recordings: cassettes full of stories and music. Every time a new box shows up, there is a bit of a celebration in the office. Everyone is excited to see what could be inside, but Tali finds the boxes heavy with responsibility too. Every cassette holds the risk of hearing a piece of culture that isn't meant for you. After a careful process of poring over the materials—hours of reading, listening and annotating—Tali is both apprehensive and curious to let a new audience hear what's on those ageing tapes.

A muffled knock and the studio door slowly opens. Ellie pops her head in and waves to get Tali's attention. 'Is this a good time?' she whispers.

'I'm not on right now, come in,' Tali says, pulling her headphones down to her neck.

'Great! This is Jack. He's new to the station, but he has family from up your way.'

Tali finds familiarity in Jack's brow and green eyes. They remind her of her uncles.

'Who's your mob, Jack?'

Tali's shoulders drop and she visibly relaxes into the desk as they play the game of tracing family trees—sharing familiar places, cousins, aunties and memories.

'I'm a musician, mostly. I've been meaning to come here for a while. I hear you might have some of my nan's stories downstairs.'

'Oh yeah? Deadly. Well, if you've got any of your own music we can play on air, drop it on my desk and I can add it to the bank.' Tali smiled. 'I'm so jealous of people who have that kind of talent.'

'Yeah, music is everything, you know. It's so powerful. I've always wanted to add some archival stuff into my songs.'

Tali nods. She has seen plenty of kids come in wanting to incorporate old material into their work. Sometimes they are reckless, or at least naive, not always aware of the danger they could get into. Teaching cultural responsibility had become part of her job since opening the station.

'I'm just about to queue up some more recordings— do you want to listen in?' she asks, gesturing towards the headphones.

Jack puts them on. Tali rearranges her playlist to pull forwards some new material that has been recently delivered to the station.

'We mostly play a mixture of local music and archival materials,' she explains. 'When new donations come in, we do our best to identify the right owners and rematriate them. If we've done as much as we can do, and we can't identify who the recording belongs to, *then* we'll put it on air. Until somebody calls in. Somebody who knows where the story belongs, and someone usually does.' Tali was proud of the practice the station had developed, broadcasting responsibly and acting on takedown requests quickly.

A crackled audio plays. Tali guesses that the recording must have been made on a train somewhere in the Goldfields. The deep voices are washed over with clacks and thumps of train tracks, with language wafting out the train window.

'What do you think? Do you recognise anything?' she asks Jack.

He opens his eyes and shakes his head.

'Nup.'

Tali shrugs. The audio team have done their best to clean up the quality of this recording. But even with the enormous advancement in restoration technology, nobody at the station has been able to identify enough words to recognise what language is being spoken.

After a minute or so of playing the recording, the phone lights up on the studio desk. Jack's eyes grow wide and Tali takes the call.

As they walk downstairs into the basement, Tali treads softly. She lifts her arms up, hands to the ceiling. Jack steps behind her a little more carelessly, his head dodging the doorframe as they descend. But he follows her suit, raising his hands.

'Sometimes families will ask for help with maintaining their own archives at home or on Country,' says Tali when they reach the bottom of the stairs. 'So we make copies and back them up here in the server room, but only with permission.'

Introducing Jack to the server room, Tali gestures towards rows of shelves that house cassettes, CDs and stacks of paper documents filed by language and family.

'We're training more young fullas like you to manage the server, so they can keep it running. I don't want to be the only one who knows how to keep these things alive.'

The machine in the middle of the floor pops and buzzes with LEDs. 'Most materials are backed up in a secondary location, but digitising items has been a long process. It's wild to think that there are racks upon racks of hard drives filled with stories and song, photographs, echoes, fragments, heavier than their file sizes, sitting down here humming away.'

Tali easily lost herself in the poetry of the archive. But she did notice Jack's eyes wandering around the room, taking in the racks of old materials, artefacts and advanced technology. She fills the silence.

'So, we don't have a universal tagging system for all these materials yet. We've made our peace with that. It isn't easy to find anything, and that's kind of the point. You need to put in some effort if you want to find a story. You can't just wander in and grab an armful, you know? You need to spend some time in here, know somebody who can show you around.' Tali spots the long feather of a karak tattooed on Jack's forearm, chuckles to herself and thinks, *That makes sense.*

'That's how it should be,' Jack says, catching her gaze.

'It's an embodied thing, you know?' Tali continues. 'It's different when an Elder comes in. They have a sense for a lot of this stuff. Even if the archive feels new and foreign, like when we first installed this server, some people say they can feel the buzzing of the machine in their bones. They know where there are stories that need to be locked tight. Stories not meant for broadcast on the air. Or not meant to reach the air at all; not meant to be spoken.'

'Yeah, I get that. I've been learning language for a few years, but I still sweat when I come across a story that isn't meant for me.'

'I know the feeling. I think that's part of listening to our old people, yeah? Deep listening and all that.' Tali turns her attention back to the tour. 'Over time, the archive evolves, too. Someone comes in with a new suggestion of how it all pieces together. Right now, the materials are separated by medium. CDs, paper, digital recordings, and so on. But each family has their own way of holding information too, informed by their ways.'

Pressed under the weight of getting this cultural work right, in the relative darkness of the server room and among the confines of shelves, Tali notices their height disparity for the first time. Jack is younger, but towers over her.

Tali reaches for a small rack hidden beside the server, where a curved wooden vessel sits scored with careful marks inside its body.

'The key for your family is carved in here. You'll be able to read it better than I can. It tells you where everything lives in the archive, and where to find your nan.'

Jack looks over the lines and circles propagating across the bark in patterns that form a blueprint of the server room.

'Thanks, Tali. I really appreciate you showing me around.'

'No worries, hey. I'll leave you to it. You can take as long as you like, I'll be here for a few more hours.'

In the afternoons, the sun produces a long column of light through the front windows stretching across the floor of the station from the desks to the doors. A path that is a beckoning reminder: *Come back out, do not stay inside for too long.* Tali walks downstairs from the studio to find Jack sitting in the listening corner.

'I've been working on something, Tali. Check this out.'

They each take a seat in two kidney-shaped chairs that face each other. Tali sets her notebook down on the small coffee table between them, takes the headphones offered by Jack and places them over her ears. There's an electronic beat and some low synth sounds, with a layer of field recordings permeating Jack's music: warm-weather cicadas, trills of evening kookaburras and the far-reaching call of the red-tailed karak. Jack's clear, low voice comes through like he's speaking from the base of her own skull:

go on post your black squares
get them likes, those shares
show up to the rallies

say you feel our pain
we can't choose this life
we are born black brown queer trans othered
we are born
politicised

It's the kind of poetry Tali loves, the kind that is infused with rage and connection. Suddenly there is a warmth growing between them. Engrossed in the song, Tali looks up to see tall flames licking the walls behind Jack, stretching towards the front windows and out into the street.

'You see it now, don't you?' Jack leans forwards, staring intently at Tali for some acknowledgement.

The bass notes from the music have turned into carbon, the snares into embers. The heat emanating from the walls melts layers of paint and charred wallpaper. It licks the ceiling in long outstretched arms. *Make Noise Boorloo* on the wall glows white and molten. Outside, waves of red and black flecks of debris tumble down the road, swallowing the sidewalk, leaving charred remains of cars in their path. Pedestrians, petrified in place, turn to charcoal and slowly crumble into the wind.

Inside the station, the flames glow red and orange, lapping at the carpet. The black and red feather tattooed on Jack's forearm glows like hot coal, and Tali notices for the first time the layer of black under his fingernails as he wipes charcoal dust from his skin. She sits in the heat, and though she may smell the burning hair creep up across her shoulders, she does not flinch.

Tali peels the headphones from her ears, now damp with sweat. The flames recede. The cars outside are clean and untouched. The people in the streets return to wandering and chattering.

'Jack… It's beautiful.'

'I knew you'd understand.'

'But you need to be careful with this.'

Jack leans back without breaking eye contact.

'Why do you act like you don't wade through marsh every morning? Pretend your feet are dry? I know you're like me. I saw your wellies in the booth, noticed you sloshing around invisible rivers in the basement.'

It's true. Every morning as she walks to the station, Tali navigates kilometres of wetlands. Everything is the way it used to look before the settlers drained the swamps. She'd never paid mind to how much it tired her, how it weighed her down. How much she wished she could move as easily through the air like everyone else did, like songs on the airwaves.

'This is my truth, Tali. I don't hide myself. I wear the soot on my skin, and I want everyone to feel the flames like I do. The heat of them.'

He's right. Tali doesn't want to take that away from him. She is scared too. Scared of how powerful he could be. Of how powerful she could be.

'And if you just played a little on the air—'

'You know I can't do that, Jack.'

It hurts her to say it. She was always talking about how the station had this incredible ability to share stories, and she was proud of the work they did. But stories can be dangerous. She worries about what that power would look like in the hands of somebody so young and full of rage. Though Tali feels like she has a responsibility to keep him in check a little, to teach him, a part of her wishes she could share his rage too. Let it all out. She sighs.

'Keep it safe, yeah? Let's talk about this later.'

Rising from her seat, Tali wanders to the other side of the room and touches the walls to ground herself. The heat still lifting, *Make Noise Boorloo* feels warm to the touch.

' S o, are you going to keep an eye on him?'
Ellie sits with Tali at the studio desk, headphones around her neck, queueing up the next set of songs. Loud piercing bird calls permeates the windows.

Tali watches the window in anticipation for the karak family to fly overhead. There was something singular about the squawk of the karak, the way their voices bellowed a call louder than their bodies appeared fit to make, a sound that carried across the wind for hundreds of metres.

Over the airwaves, the station plays her own music for the first time. A story of history and archive and truth-telling. Tali had poured messes of herself, from throat to belly, into this music and it made her feel lighter. All the hard work and responsibility that she had been carrying for this place, turned to waves in the wind.

Beneath the birds, stretching across the city, Tali watches the movement of bewildered pedestrians walking through ankle-to-knee-deep wetlands, thick with bullrushes. The street slows down.

Strangler Fig

Aisling Smith

Anita looks to the winter sky, bright and pearlescent overhead. *Beautiful* is the only word she can conjure, and she recoils. She remembers reading a tutor's rebuke scrawled in the margins of a story she submitted to an undergraduate creative writing workshop: *Never use adjectives like 'beautiful' unless you are being ironic, it's unimaginative.* Anita had taken the edict to heart.

Think harder, she urges herself. What colour stretches above her head? *White.* The weather? *Cloudy.* The temperature? *Cold.* But that's where it stops—the descriptions stall, the metaphors will not be coaxed. It's Lego-block language, clumsy and simple. *Embarrassing.*

She tries to pinpoint when it happened—if she knew that, maybe she could figure out the rest of it and cobble together a solution. Was it a sudden disappearance or a slow dwindling? Did they fade away or flee? A skein of cotton wool stretches across her memory of the past three years.

She'd been a different person before. But that version feels like the half-forgotten image of someone she went to school with. Someone she can't quite remember enough to miss.

She is sitting in the park on a Sunday afternoon. Soon she will return home—not to free dive for a new poem or work on her half-finished novel as she used to do—but to an empty apartment and the canned laughter of a Netflix sitcom.

On Monday morning, Anita sits in the Acorn Property Development office with the two others on the marketing team and writes copy to send to their supervisor, Kathryn. *Embrace a luxury lifestyle. Raise sunset toasts to CBD views. There's no place you'd rather be.* They roll their eyes at each other over their laptops, but the job has a rhythm to it. She can recycle phrases she has used before, so no one notices that she is an exoskeleton. She has fooled them all with her freshly ironed shirt and the GIFs she posts in Teams.

On her break, she checks the footy-tipping chart and makes black coffee in her KeepCup. At lunch, she eats with her teammates and shares small, irrelevant details from her weekend.

She used up most of her sick leave earlier in the year after the breakup, telling Kathryn that she was 'having a hard time'.

'You can talk to me if you want to,' Kathryn had offered, though she had been visibly relieved when Anita had nodded her thanks and left the office in silence.

When Anita returned from her two weeks off, everyone wanted to know if she felt better.

'You bet,' she had chirped and made her mouth smile.

But this week is special: on Friday, her brother Anton arrives for a long weekend—and he is bringing little Ivy. Caroline, pregnant with baby number two, will remain in Perth, not wanting to take more time off work ahead of her upcoming maternity leave.

'You're only staying three nights? We haven't seen you for ages,' Anita had complained when Anton called to tell her.

'You sound like Mum,' he groaned. But they both laughed because a comparison to their mother was a compliment.

'I can't wait to see you,' she had whispered and was horrified to hear her voice become croaky. There had been a pause at the other end and, unusual for Anton, no jibe had followed.

'Me too, Ani,' he'd eventually told her, sounding both embarrassed and sincere. She managed to hold it together until she got off the phone.

She had added the dates to her calendar and, now that it draws close, she keeps opening the app on her phone just to see the little banner on the screen: *Anton & Ivy visiting*.

On Tuesday, Marc invites her over for dinner. She takes a rosemary focaccia to his tiny flat and chooses a Spotify playlist (The War on Drugs) as he adds spices to saucepans. Before long, the scent of cumin fills the apartment.

Anita watches him from the sofa. She waited eight months before dating again. Maybe it should have been longer. With each new man, she had worn an A-line skirt and performed a version of herself that was not a lie and yet not the truth either. She became an abridged Anita, with both her troubles and ambitions redacted. Digestible. Palatable. Inoffensive. And, truth be told, most of her dates only wanted an audience—to see their image mirrored back to them in another's eyes and hear the echo of laughter at their jokes.

On their first date, she and Marc had eaten pain au chocolat in a cafe. She'd been oddly touched that he hadn't noticed the pastry flakes that had fallen onto his shirt. He wasn't charming or glittery—she liked that. He chatted to her about working as an engineer, while she'd told him about her writing process. They'd traded tales of contented childhoods and first-date war stories.

Marc still doesn't know the full story about her and the ex. She gave a simplified version on their fourth date, and he'd squeezed her hand sympathetically across the restaurant table.

'That's awful,' he'd murmured, his voice low. 'Guys like that are fucking pricks.'

He hadn't offered anything more. They hadn't discussed it again, though sometimes she sees questions in his eyes. If he is waiting for her to share more of the story, it will never come.

She wants to be asked. She doesn't want to be asked.

But Marc calls when he says he will and volunteers at the Red Cross shop on the weekends. If they stay together, she knows that he will propose to her one day and stay faithful to his wedding vows. His simple, straightforward world beckons her. He might not seek out her depths, but he won't inflict darkness upon her either.

After dinner, they have sex in his double bed. Marc struggles to locate her clitoris—he paws arrhythmically between her legs until she takes pity on him and replaces his hand with her own. Her fingers soon lose their momentum as his body rises above her and she is submerged in his shadow. Then what her body feels is irrelevant. Her seaweed limbs are marooned on the bed, and she drifts above—she is flotsam bobbing on algal foam. She is alone in an endless sea, watching herself drift further and further from the shore of herself. Ultimately, it doesn't matter that he does not know how to give her pleasure because she can't feel her body anyway.

When she re-emerges into her own skin, she can taste the brine of their sweat on her lips and feel the moisture of his exertion on her waterlogged body. There's a discarded condom wrapper on the floor and she falls asleep watching the foil catch the streetlight through a gap in the curtain.

Her therapist finds the floating away concerning when they discuss it in their session a couple of days later. He uses formal, diagnostic words for it, though his face is soft and sad.

'I'm concerned about you, Anita,' he says.

She frowns, puzzled. *I'm not concerned, so why should you be?*

'It doesn't bother me,' she tells him. 'I really don't care.'

'That,' he replies, 'is the problem.'

Maybe he's right, she reflects as she sits at her laptop that evening with her fingers immobile on the keys and her novel as unfinished as ever. Nothing comes. She is a shell shucked of an oyster. Then again, how could she possibly write when she can't even connect with her body—when she's untethered from it, leaving it behind? How could anything flow from her under those conditions?

Silty memories drip across her mind unfiltered. It's bore water, not safe to drink. Her heartbeat is rapid. She startles at unexpected noises. At work, her mind slides away from the sentences on her page, and when people talk to her, she watches their mouths make shapes without hearing the sounds.

Despite all this, she continues once a fortnight to sit in an armchair next to a lush monstera and learns about attachment styles and trauma bonding. For fifty minutes, she is soothed. For fifty minutes, she is audacious enough to believe that she will, in fact, be okay. She exits with her shoulders back and her chin parallel to the ground, carrying the fledgling knowledge with her like a talisman.

But these days her mind is a sieve, and hour by hour that warm confidence seeps away. The knowledge that seemed so clear in that neat rectangular room is impossible to hold onto.

Somehow, she ends up alone in the sea once again.

She still thinks of the ex, and her traitorous fingers click through to his social media. He's dating someone new too, and they look happy. Is he different with her? She's younger than Anita, with a pretty face and an easy smile.

He'd once just been a face on an app. She'd met him for Friday night drinks. The two hours she'd intended to spend with him had somehow melted into five. He was less handsome than he imagined himself to be but resplendent with charisma—he knew how to draw out a laugh from even the grumpiest soul.

Why is Anita's mind even now ensnared by memories of his sweetness? She can picture the earnestness in his blue eyes when he told her he loved her, his big hands cradling a cup of tea for her in the morning and the infectiousness of his quirky grin. So much of their time together had been good.

They hadn't been together for long when he asked her to move in. He'd made the offer so readily, with an eagerness that could only be evidence of his love matching hers. Her friends had long since celebrated their hens' nights and weddings—replaced now by baby showers and christenings. It was Anita's turn.

They found a small townhouse to rent, close enough to the city that they could both ride their bikes to work. When the key was theirs and the removalist trucks had gone, she had wandered through the house, trailing her hand over their belongings—her tennis racquet next to his golf clubs and their toothbrushes in the same ceramic mug, bristles touching. The future was golden and glowing.

And yet she spent her thirty-first birthday at the hospital. The trio of women manning the MRI scanner had become gentler with her when they read her chart and her name was instantly softened to *sweetheart*.

'Don't you worry, sweetheart, this is going to be easy.'

They asked her if she was claustrophobic and she had shaken her head. They warned her that the machine would be noisy, but lying in that metal tube, she found herself unbothered by it. The women had spoken to her periodically: *You're doing great, honey. We're almost done.* Anita kept her face very still and blinked into glare the above her as she felt tears suddenly overflow from the corner of her eyes and move downwards into her hair.

A few days later, her GP showed her the ghostly images. So that was her brain. Displayed on the big monitor, it looked like a shadowy fig or a pomelo sliced open.

'The scan doesn't show any abnormalities, despite the concussion,' Dr Begam told her. 'The symptoms you're experiencing don't appear to have a physical origin. But I'll refer you to a specialist service for some help navigating your relationship—you know none of this is okay, right?'

'Yes,' Anita said. 'I know. We're not together anymore. I ended it after it happened.' Though her belongings were still in the house and her name on the lease.

Dr Begam had nodded, a tide of relief washing over her face.

Anita decided not to mention how much she missed him.

Trauma changes the brain, they say. But it's not just the way his closed fist colliding with her skull endangered the soft, vulnerable organ encased within it.

They had lived a palimpsest life together, with his reality stencilled over hers. His rages had left holes in the plasterboard walls and destroyed furniture. When they walked together down the street, his eyes would flicker between the taut bodies of other women and her own softness, his mouth narrowing— followed by the comparisons. Back then, he'd only let her eat steamed vegetables.

Words had always come easily to the ex. Even now, his putdowns remain embedded in her flesh.

You're lucky to have me.

Nobody will ever love you as much as I do.

Shut your mouth.

You're nothing without me.

Before him, Anita had fallen asleep easily. But now habitual nightmares catapult her into wakefulness at three in the morning, her mind choppy and storming. She has read countless blog posts on sleep hygiene but still picks up her phone and strokes her thumb over its screen, letting the blue light bathe her eyeballs.

When she falls asleep again hours later, she dreams of a trip she'd taken with the ex to Byron Bay in the early days. Seventeen hours in the car, with the aircon chapping her lips and her head lolling against the shuddering window. Though the countryside beyond the window was everchanging, her attention had been fixed on his nose in profile, the line of his jaw and the drivers' tan deepening across his pale forearm. As the scenery turned tropical, they'd pulled over to stretch their legs and follow one of the short walks marked on their crumpled paper map.

'This one,' he'd directed, pointing to the gully trail. 'It's half an hour.'

They'd walked in silent separateness beneath the lush canopy until they reached the small wooden platform at the end of the track. There, he'd wrapped his arms around her from behind—*strong muscly arms*, she'd thought giddily as he kissed her temple. They stood in the shade of a gigantic tree that stretched upwards towards the sky, with a twisted ropey form.

'I think that's actually two trees,' he'd said when she pointed it out.

Sure enough, she could see it—the roots of one plant engulfing the other, wrapped around it like a protective shield. *Ficus watkinsiana*, the small cursive plaque had read. It was only later that she learned the common name for the plant. Union, she had thought dreamily at the time.

'That's you and me, baby,' he'd murmured, as if reading her mind. 'Together forever.'

Ficus watkinsiana. Strangler fig.

F riday finally comes around. Anton texts her to let her know that he and Ivy have arrived safely, and Anita feels a rush of nervous relief. It'll just be the five of them at Mum and Dad's for dinner this evening.

Walking up to the front door, she can hear Ivy's soprano. As soon as she enters the house, Anton pulls her into a tight bear hug.

'How are you, Ani?' he asks, peering down into her face, one arm still around her shoulders.

They're close when they see each other, but that isn't often these days. Anton is impossible to communicate with electronically, with his monosyllabic texts and delayed replies. For a moment, she wants to tell him about everything—the ex, the medical appointments and the lost words. But Mum is on her way over with bhaji for them, and Anita doesn't know where to begin anyway.

'I'm fine, Ant,' she settles on. It's true enough. Or at least sometimes true. 'How are you?'

'Tired,' he says, with a grumble of laughter.

Anita smiles. This is every parent's answer. She doesn't blame him—Ivy is indefatigable. She twirls around the living room in a circle skirt, always on her tiptoes, humming to herself. She trails her hand over the mantelpiece and whispers things to the photographs in their seashell frames. The siblings watch her from the kitchen as their parents put together a feast. They share the cooking and can't help going overboard when Anton visits. Anita doesn't need to look at the kitchen counter to know that there will be bebinca for dessert.

'She's a good kid,' Mum says.

'Beautiful child,' Dad agrees.

Anton beams with pride.

All their faces are soft and serene—except for Anita, who is suddenly breathless. What kind of world is this for Ivy? *Treat her well, keep her safe, don't hurt her.* She wants to scream the words aloud, although she doesn't even know who she is addressing. Beside her, the other three are laughing, their teeth flashing white against brown skin.

From meeting in Panaji as students studying economics, Mum and Dad have grown together over the thirty-nine years since their marriage. They are two tall trees, side by side, their boughs reaching up to the sky, separate but parallel, and rooted from the same place. They made it seem so simple: Respect your elders. Family matters. Love your spouse.

Their gentle home life had not prepared their children for a world where love wasn't always enough. Although Anton is three years older, he has escaped many of the harder lessons that Anita recently learned. With his wife Caroline, he has smoothly continued what their parents taught them.

Anita is so caught up in her thoughts she startles when she feels a small tug on her T-shirt. Ivy has snuck up beside her.

'Race me, Tia!' the child demands.

Anita's legs feel heavy and her lower back aches. But she is the 'fun aunt', and Ivy's face is beseeching, her dark eyes and long eyelashes are just like Anton's. Anita sighs and lets Ivy lead her out of the house and down the back stairs into the garden. *What's the etiquette here? Am I supposed to let her win?* she wonders apprehensively.

'Okay, munchkin. To the tree and back?' There's a magnolia at the far end of the yard.

Ivy nods.

Mum, Dad and Anton have come out onto the verandah to watch.

'I'll do the countdown,' Anton says as aunt and niece take their places on the edge of the garden bed. 'Ready…set…GO!'

Ivy bolts off—she is surprisingly speedy. Her mousey ponytail, mixed with Caroline's blonde, streams behind her in a wisp. Anita presses into her quadriceps and propels her body after Ivy. Now that she's in motion, she's moving quickly herself. Ivy is ahead, but her small legs can't match Anita's, and they reach the tree at the same time.

'You have to *touch* the tree!' Ivy reprimands, and Anita has to double back slightly to brush her hands over the bark. Even so, she overtakes Ivy on the return.

'Come on, kid!' she calls over her shoulder and slows her pace so that she is just ahead. Then, in the last few metres, she lets Ivy dash ahead.

'I won!' the little girl shrieks. 'Avó, did you see?'

'I did,' Mum applauds, delicate bangles shaking at her wrists.

'Well done,' Anton smiles, though he raises his eyebrows at his sister. 'You shouldn't have done that,' he admonishes Anita quietly as she ascends the stairs to return to the house. 'It's not good for her. She needs to learn how to lose and be gracious in defeat. I don't want her to be one of those overconfident kids who've always been allowed to believe they're the best.'

Anita snorts. 'Clearly, you've never been a teenage girl. She'll have enough people bringing her down soon enough.'

Anton scowls. 'Spare me the feminist rant. Just don't let her win next time, okay?'

Anita shrugs and goes to the fridge to find the riesling.

Her heart is still thumping from the sprint—pounding against her chest, in fact. The nape of her neck is humid. Opening the fridge, she is aware of the gust of cold air on her skin.

Gelid. The word darts across her mind from nowhere and, startled, she stands still. It's one of the lost fragments. Will any other vocabulary return in its wake? She waits. Long beats stretch out in silence until the fridge, still ajar, beeps in irritation. But nothing else comes. The word is a solitary minnow, escaping a scoop net back into a stream. Almost as soon as it appeared, it has passed out of sight again—and yet, for a moment, it was there.

As she pours the wine, she hears her breath becoming a little shallow, feels it high in her ribcage. The blood is cycling around her body and her lungs balloon with oxygen. Everything is just as it should be.

More than that—for the first time in such a long time, it occurs to her that she is here too. She is not hovering above her body or marooned at sea. She is here, immersed, embodied. Here, with her hammering heart and heated skin.

Just here—and nowhere else.

Short Shorts and Other Short Stories

Ennis Ćehić

1

Everybody has a quirk. This is his.

As the Zoom meeting draws to a close, he orchestrates his exit with precision. 'Bye, bye,' he says, his hand waving at the camera, eyes fixed on the grid of faces before him. One by one, he watches his colleagues' screens wink out until only his own virtual reflection remains.

Here he pauses, but only briefly, scrutinising his profile as he pushes himself away from the desk. Standing up, he scrunches his shoulders and completes a quick succession of knee-ups before turning off the lights and sitting back down.

From underneath the chair, he retrieves a cushion to sit on. Keeping his back straight yet relaxed, he adjusts the screen to emit only a soft glow from his laptop. Inhaling deeply, he fills his lungs with the stale air of the room, then exhales slowly, observing his breath leave his body in the reflection. Then he closes his eyes and repeats the process—again and again.

Back then, when this started, he simply enjoyed being the last person left. There was nothing more to it. Now this quirk has become a ritual. A moment of private osmosis that some might call meditation, others escapism. For him, it's a chance to take hold of something mysterious—the peculiar energy that remains in the ether of every Zoom meeting room.

Breathing is paramount. It's the way in to this virtual phenomenon, but thoughts and distractions often arise. He's realised that he can't judge himself for getting distracted; it's a normal part of the method. Like any meditation, it takes practice to reach the right state of symbiosis.

What he's after is the lingering thoughts and emotions left behind by others: remnants of interesting insights, shreds of personal intuition, fragments of valuable viewpoints. At first, he had no clue how to sponge up this valuable energy. Now, with each breath, he can feel the transfer. It spikes the neurons in his brain, tingling with new ideas.

Usually it's over when thoughts and distractions resurface that can no longer be pushed aside. Today, it is the rumble of construction work happening nearby. He can hear the beeping of a truck backing up. The drilling and sawing of machinery and power tools.

With his mind charged up like a battery, he opens his eyes. The soft glow from his laptop doesn't feel so soft anymore; the light appears brighter. He drops back into his chair and stretches his neck slowly. Beside his laptop a worn diary lies open, its pages filled with dates, times and cryptic numbers arranged in neat columns. He grabs it and marks today's entry with a ballpoint pen: *021.*

Sometimes he wonders how he's the only one attuned to this. It's not some misguided fantasy; it definitely happens.

He has proof: twenty-one sessions have resulted in two promotions, and no one knows how he managed it, and so quickly. It's why he has to hurry. He has to find a more lucrative way to capitalise on this virtual energy, for someone else is bound to stumble upon it sooner or later.

2

I t was Dionysus who heard my incessant cries.

He said my tears had kept him awake, and had decided for the first time in over three thousand years to come down to earth for a chat with a human being.

When he arrived on my porch, he brought with him a decent bottle of Richebourg Grand Cru and two stemless wine glasses. 'Young man,' he said, 'I am here to assuage your fractured heart.'

I was accustomed to the idyllic depictions—the beautiful, nude youth with a wreath of vines crowning his head, or the dignified elderly man with a white beard—but before me stood a small, fat man with a reddish face and a tattered cloth around his waist.

I motioned for him to sit down, and he slumped onto the chair across from me. He opened the bottle of wine, poured some into the glasses, and said cheers. I offered him a cigarette. When we lit up, I realised what he had really come down here for. Like me, he wanted to know why love will forever remain the core subject of human existence.

3

On this trip, all he wanted to buy was one pair of short shorts. Just one.

But the pair he thought were perfect turned out to be too long, almost to the knees. In the mirror inside the store where he'd tried them on, they had looked good though. The light organic twill cotton was breezy around his legs. The black colour emphasised his muscular thighs—even the passing attendant thought so. He ran his fingers over the material, felt the soft texture of the weave, and looked back at his reflection in the mirror. He felt a fleeting rush of euphoria. *Have a pair of shorts ever looked this good on me?* he asked himself. Just then, the attendant passed by again, echoing his thoughts with another compliment.

Outside the store, the rush of euphoria soon vanished. In its place, guilt arrived. He looked down ashamedly at the shopping bag in his hand. This was supposed to be the year of being frugal. The year he'd become a real conscious shopper, so what the hell was he doing? He had lasted eight months without purchasing a single new item. But here he was, on the first day of vacation, the flippant and frivolous spender he'd always been.

He continued to walk down a narrow lane until he eyed a cafe just before the Piazza del Duomo. The cafe's colourful tablecloths, adorned with Moorish heads, bright lemons and swirly patterns, beckoned invitingly. Its patio overlooked the corner of the Syracuse Cathedral, and from there he could watch people enter the suntrap of the central square.

It was his first time in Ortigia. The tiny island, surrounded by the turquoise waters of the Mediterranean, had impressed him immediately upon arrival. He felt calmed by its sandstone facades, balconies adorned with summer-ripe flower boxes and cafes spilling out onto the sun-soaked pavements.

'Buongiorno,' said an elderly waiter.

'Espresso, please,' he said without attempting to order in Italian.

His mind was too occupied, too furious at itself. Was it really justifiable? *Our planet was burning!* he reminded himself as he wiped the sweat from his brow and looked out onto Piazza del Duomo.

It really was a showpiece, a long rectangular square that sits on what was once Syracuse's ancient acropolis, surrounded by baroque palazzi. He glared at a woman in a shiny polyester dress, its garish neon colour clashing with the surroundings, her legs weighed down by three boutique shopping bags. It kindled rage in him. He wished the overstuffed shopping bags were filled with less ugly items. *Reckless habits,* he thought, trying to recall the positive outcomes of conscious shopping. Angrily, he started to list the outcomes in his head but couldn't remember much else except reduced resource consumption and lower carbon emissions.

The espresso arrived.

On the saucer, beside the teaspoon, he found a complimentary biscuit. He bit into it. He knew the guilt was still there, and not because he had bought the pair of shorts but because he knew he'd still look for the other pair—the pair he was really after.

He took a sip of the coffee and glanced around. From here, he was planning to head east to wander around Giudecca, the ancient Jewish quarter, then he'd make his way back to Corso Giacomo Matteotti, the main shopping stretch. The afternoon would be reserved for swimming at the Diana nel Forte beach, which was close to his hotel.

He got up, paid for his coffee, and decided to walk south instead, through Duomo. It wasn't yet ten o'clock, but the temperature was rising fast. He could feel the back of his neck burning as he walked through the square.

He had always loved summer, but recent summers scared him. They had been scaring him for a while, actually, with the Earth's temperature rising and extreme heatwaves becoming too frequent worldwide. That's how all this personal frugality came about, really. For him, climate change was irrefutable. Weren't these wildfires evidence enough? He'd never been a penny-pincher, but he had to act. And since he'd always been a reckless consumer, buying less stuff was the best way to start.

He had almost cancelled his vacation to Sicily. Just a few days before his arrival, a fire had reached the passenger terminal of Catania Airport. Firefighters fought the blaze for hours before gaining control. The aftermath left the airport in chaos. With parts of the terminal scorched, temporary structures had to be erected, causing delays for all flights.

He drove out of the airport in a rental, stunned by the whole ordeal. For a long stretch of the trip to Ortigia, all he could see was blackened land, smoke still rising off burnt trees and bushes along the highway.

But here he was nevertheless, slowing down his walk, battling old consumerist tendencies in front of a menswear store. He had turned onto a narrow alleyway pebbled with cute, shaded restaurants, so how did he get here? He must've taken a turn absent-mindedly, for this street seemed to be lined with nothing but boutique fashion stores.

A pair of cream shorts with a water-repellent stretch fabric hanging in the window caught his eye. They looked thinner and shorter. He walked into the store and asked the attendant for a size M to try on. He wanted to get the whole thing over and done with as quickly as possible. There was that beach to go to.

In the mirror, the shorts sat way higher than the other ones, above his knees. They exposed his thighs beautifully, just like he had first imagined they would. Just like he saw on that hot influencer on Instagram who always wore short shorts.

He rubbed his fingers over the fabric; it was smooth and slightly slick. The cream colour felt right against his skin, vibrant yet unpretentious, perfect for this Sicilian summer. On the label, he read that thanks to the unique finish of the material (which was made from recycled plastic bottles) these shorts had quick-drying properties. This got him excited. It meant that he could go straight from the water to that cute trattoria and be dry by the time he sat down, ready to enjoy his pranzo.

He wished he had come here earlier, before the other store, but it didn't matter now. These shorts were it—definitely. There was nothing else he needed. This was the pair he envisioned wearing on this trip. When he took them off and folded them, he couldn't help admiring the craftsmanship and attention to detail, from the stitching to the subtle logo embroidered on the back pocket.

At the counter, the attendant's excitement about the purchase only fuelled his own desire.

'Special, sir. Duo for uno,' the attendant said, holding up two fingers to emphasise the deal. He understood but tried to play it cool. Deep down, he knew a bargain like this was too good to pass up, especially for a garment that's supposed to embody the essence of his vacation.

'It's okay, just the one,' he said, trying to resist the urge as he reached for his wallet. But the sales attendant, sensing his hesitation, was persistent. He motioned for him to return to the shorts section, repeating 'duo for uno' with a persuasive tone. Reluctantly, he followed, his eyes scanning over the array of colours: deep green, rich burgundy, sunny yellow—each colour reflecting the island's varied hues.

Outside the store, he felt surprisingly satisfied. No, he felt like he had lucked out completely with this deal. His Sicilian vacation could start properly now. But where was he? He looked at Google Maps on his iPhone, and the map indicated that he was a fifteen-minute walk from his hotel.

He began to follow the map, but he could feel it nagging at him, like a reminder tapping on his shoulder. Three pairs? Wasn't that excessive? When he felt the two shopping bags bump against his thigh, he couldn't help but think of the woman in the shiny polyester dress, and was embarrassed. The extravagance was a pure betrayal of his own principles. But really, was he straying so far from his original plan for the year? To buy less didn't mean buy nothing! Did it? The first pair of shorts was an amazing fit, and these two were a bargain.

He picked up pace and followed the shade through every street. Maybe he could wear with the cream shorts that nice floral Hawaiian shirt his mother bought him? Or that tie-dye linen shirt he picked up in Madrid last year? That would pair well with the first shorts he'd bought. He couldn't wait to change and head out for dinner somewhere nice. Maybe that seafood place he'd read about near his hotel.

With his mind racing like this, he reached into his pocket for a cigarette. He stopped underneath the shaded awning of an art gallery. On the corner of the building was a small fountain where tourists filled their water bottles. Although he was thirsty, he had already lit up. He smoked and idly scrolled through his social feed, pausing when a new post appeared from the hot influencer who always wore short shorts. The guy flaunted a new pair—green nylon shorts matched with a grey woollen long sleeve, low-cut socks and brown penny loafers. The shorts were superb, but the outfit irritated him. The combination was weird, and he felt like the guy was trying too hard. He took a sharp puff of his cigarette before raising his eyes from the iPhone. And there, in front of him, on a mannequin, beside another mannequin, he spotted the same pair of shorts from the post. *It couldn't be?* He shook his head in disbelief. He laughed, a little manically. A little too hysterically. He had obviously strolled in front of this shop window absent-mindedly, but he didn't expect this. He examined the shorts on the influencer's post and the shorts on the mannequin closely. 'Fucking hell,' he exclaimed. They were undoubtedly the same shorts featured in the post.

Wasn't this the kind of thing that only happened online? One minute you're thinking about slippers, and the next they're for sale in your feed? No, he wasn't going to go in and try them on; that would be ridiculous. He was just going to look at them from a distance while he smoked his cigarette, but as he crushed the moistened butt with his foot, he found himself walking into the store carelessly. Just to have a look, you know, not to buy, just to feel the fabric—and sure enough they were wonderful to touch. He rubbed the nylon a few times between his fingers, and then suddenly he was in front of the mirror wearing them, and oh my god—the fit was as surprising as the coincidence. These shorts flared out slightly on the sides, unlike the more straight-legged ones he had just bought.

No, he couldn't deny the pull of them. He hesitated to admit it, but they had a certain destiny about them, didn't they? *A kind of providence.* He had forgotten, Ortigia was the mythological home of heroes and deities. Ancient gods were fucking with him, weren't they? Maybe Artemis—she was born here. Was he being punished for aiding and abetting these Sicilian wildfires with his torrent of consumerism? He looked at himself in the mirror. At his hand gliding over the fabric of the green shorts. He chuckled, and then it all happened.

One moment he was in front of the mirror, the next he was at the counter, tapping his credit card on the machine. Then he found himself outside the store, lighting another cigarette. He glanced at the sun, uncertain of the time, before noticing three overstuffed bags swinging against his thigh. But it wasn't just the bags; he felt the jostle of other shoppers, heard their laughter mingling with the sounds of happy vacationers. Taking a deep breath, he observed the bustling strip he was walking along, filled with people enjoying themselves. He longed to feel as carefree as they did, but when he reached his hotel room and saw the four pairs of shorts laid out on his bed, he felt sick to his stomach. They weren't fashion statements. They were vile announcements of his participation in a system that prioritised material possessions over environmental responsibility.

He reached for a bottle of mineral water from the mini-fridge and drank it down rapidly, sucking on the bottle's end until every last drop was gone. He questioned why he hadn't quenched his thirst at the water fountain earlier. The rush of hydration eased him, until he glanced back at the bed, where the pairs of brand-new shorts lay with tags still attached. *How much water had been used to produce them?* he wondered.

He looked it up on a sustainability website owned by GAP: 4,255 litres. 'Fuck,' he muttered, storming off to grab his wallet from the shopping bags. Emptying its contents onto the bed, he noticed the crumpled receipts among the banknotes. With a heavy sigh, he slumped down next to the heap, letting out a loud yawn, before stretching out on the bed to read about fashion on his phone. About its contribution to climate change, plastic pollution and violence. He went deep, into the wormhole. On Instagram, he scrolled through his feed, checked his DMs, scrolled again, then replied to a DM. Time passed in this manner, as it always does, slipping away unnoticed. Outside, the afternoon heat had died down, clouds formed, and it grew darker. A bird swooped onto his balcony railing from a nearby tree, though he remained oblivious as he yawned again and stared up at the ceiling.

And like this, irritable and sad, he fell asleep.

He slept for a while, to almost nine o'clock. When he woke, he felt resolute. Tenacious would be the right word, actually. In front of the mirror, he tried on each of the shorts with various outfits. He settled on wearing the last pair he purchased and combined these green shorts with a grey woollen long-sleeve, low-cut socks and brown penny loafers, all of which still had their tags attached. Before he left, he was certain he had settled on another matter; tomorrow, he would return none of them.

4

'Speak to me, you stones!' pleaded Goethe to the lifeless ruins of Rome in 1786.

'Give me a break!' pleaded I to the same ruins two hundred and thirty-eight years later.

5

After taking a deep breath, Esma coughed up her past into her hand.

The small, gruesome matter wiggled around on her palm, its texture warm and slimy against her skin. She inspected its organic form, feeling a mix of disgust and relief as she stared at the physical manifestation of her history. Each wriggle seemed to echo the journey of her life. She dropped it into her half-empty glass of pinot noir and watched it swirl in the wine with approval.

Straight away, she motioned to the waiter for the bill. When he came and placed the wireless machine before her, Esma moved the glass aside; she didn't want the waiter to see her past swirling in the wine. She tapped her Visa card and waited for the payment to process, then grabbed her jacket. As she dashed for the door, she heard him—the waiter.

'Hey,' he said. 'You can't leave your past here.'

'It's okay,' said Esma as she opened the door and stepped out of the restaurant.

'But it's your past,' he said running after her. 'You'll need it.'

Further up the street, Esma came to a stop. She straightened her posture and took a few deep breaths to calm herself. A smile appeared on her face as she gradually regained her composure. Retrieving her iPhone from her pocket, she unlocked the screen and gazed at the date and time. Then she positioned her fingers and took a screenshot.

It was nine-thirty on a Tuesday.

6

They could be bourgeois if only they ate chives.

But they can't eat chives, for chives make them sick. An intense abdominal pain in the area between the bottom of their ribs and their pelvis arrives each time they eat chives. Sometimes the aches and cramps persist severely for hours.

They feel sad, for they really would like to be bourgeois. But to be bourgeois, they have been told by the bourgeoisie, they had to eat chives. This confused them—surely their noble lineage was enough? They were sons and daughters of illustrious European families. Their ancestry carved the path for constitutional governments. They had once propounded liberalism and even overthrew England's feudal order.

The bourgeoisie acknowledged their noble lineage but emphasised the importance of chive appreciation. 'It is the precondition to joining our society,' they said.

Legend has it that centuries ago, during a lavish banquet in the Marais, a waiter accidentally dropped a single chive onto the dining table before all the guests. Rather than scorn the poor waiter, the gracious host, a successful banker by the name of Laurent Livière, picked it up and demanded everyone's attention.

'Ladies and gentlemen,' said Mr Livière. 'This little herb… doesn't it bear an aristocratic demeanour? Look how it adorns our delicately plated dishes. It's a flourish reserved for the most discerning palates. It punctuates our culinary landscape with a subtle yet unmistakable flavour, a true nod to our epicurean pleasures. Indeed…to savour chives is to partake in a ritual of opulence, a testament to the exquisite refinement of the bourgeoisie.'

The crowd roared and clapped. They saluted their host, raised him up on their shoulders and proclaimed that all future members of the bourgeoisie must possess an unwavering fondness for this herb to be considered worthy of their lofty status. This—the bourgeois were told—is how the chive appreciation started.

'We have the appreciation, we just don't have the stomachs!' they pleaded to the bourgeoisie. 'Look at us. Can't you see we are today's spirit of capitalism? We have the attitude and brashness of digital-age aristocracy. We have the snootiness and brutal cliquishness of the "in" crowd. We collect art not because it is good but because it is expensive!'

'Let us in,' they demanded. They kept on pleading like this, this intrepid group of social climbers, pounding at the doors of the bourgeoisie, who with time, paid them less and less attention. Until one day, hearing the knocks fading, an elite member of the bourgeoisie said, 'Maybe we should let them in.'

The others looked at him inquisitively. 'If they can't handle a little discomfort for the sake of refinement,' they said, 'are they truly ready?'

'None of us were,' said the elite member, tapping his paunch coolly. 'It might be time they finally learn the meaning of risk and reward.'

7

The stuff she ordered online did not bring her happiness.

It annoyed her, because she thought it would. When it didn't, she reminded herself that she was no quitter. She would try again. And again. Eventually, the retail therapy would work. It had to. Maybe sixty, maybe eighty more times would do it. And then—she would finally be at peace.

Bushfire

Lee Hana

The flames were coming.

Paperback was finally forced to accept this fact when three young Sundowners appeared in his yard one summer morning. There had been an early mist on the river. Squatting, they had watched him as he watched them from the verandah. It was hard to believe. He must have convinced himself it was all just a story. The ash smeared beneath their silent eyes made the boys look frightened.

They didn't want to talk, so Paperback beckoned them inside for ice that he shaved from the cold box and sweetened with apple juice. Then he put them to work carrying his most valued books down the stairs. In a panic, he'd thought to move the library to the old grain silo where masonry might offer some protection.

But now he wasn't sure. The river had never been this low and everything was so damned dry. Tall eucalypts, each a potential torch, stood beside the broken silo and a remnant of iron tracks. He'd read once that you could forecast an unseen train by placing an ear to the track. But that required an unbroken line—and a train.

Lord, why had he not prepared? This had all been foretold, even if it wasn't written down. The gods may not exist, but faith was real. He'd read once that madness was like a wildfire—or contagion.

This was all too fast. His mind wasn't ready. The body, suddenly, so tired.

And yet he could have looked anywhere and found the blackened trunks. They stood there, deeper in the bush, behind heat-curled foliage. Cockatoos screeched. Somehow he'd let an important tradition slip. Fuel had built up. Had it been forty years already since Father dragged the family into the river as the sky caught fire? He remembered a billion sparks flying to join the stars, and then charred ruins, scorched animals floating in the river, tears clearing channels down Mother's ash-blackened face...

They worked all afternoon. The next day, Paperback felt he should return the boys back to town. Only after they'd set off did he acknowledge the sinking feeling inside: this would be his only chance to petition for exemption. All morning they followed the river, the cart rolling drowsy over dried leaves and dirt. Gum trees wilted above the yellow grass. The air was resinous, ready to ignite.

The boys resumed their urchin nature as soon as they entered the town proper. 'Your ice tastes like fish!' they cried, and he roared at them as they disappeared into anonymous alleys of slat-wood tenements. The boys gave him heart: in school these children sat straight as sticks, mindlessly reciting for hours on end.

Paperback went to find a merchant who owed him some money. The man had always been fair in their dealings, interested as much by swapping news as preserves and salt.

He also kept an eye out for stray books that Paperback might want—surely this man had an open mind. But when Paperback walked into the gloom of the warehouse, he became alarmed. Surplus might be a sin for these people, but trade was tolerated. After all, who was perfect? Paperback had always been happy to take produce in exchange for the salted fish he brought. But today he found the trader had renounced it all and wore ash on his face. The floor had been cleared of stock, which could be glimpsed in a great pile out back like a bonfire waiting for a spark.

He had difficulty getting the merchant's attention—the man was involved in some kind of complicated ablution, shedding layers of worldliness. His head was shaved and he wasn't even interested in the ancient magazine of copulative arts proffered as a gift. Before Paperback left, though, he managed to extract the name of a contact in the Sundowners' ruling council.

Government sat on top of the hill where it oversaw the sprawling settlement. From this vantage point, Paperback wiped his brow and looked down at the streets. By far the most prominent structures were the schools, which stood tall among ramshackle clapboard houses. *Factories of ignorance,* he thought sourly.

Sweeping cement stairs were the only permanent element of the Great Hall of the Sun—a relic from a previous era. Paperback climbed them to a capacious yet simple timber building standing perhaps five storeys tall. *A big bloody matchbox.* Locusts made an incessant din.

Paperback went inside, took off his hat before the concierge and invoked the name he'd been given. Then he waited, sweating, until shadows began to creep into the unpainted lobby, empty but for the bare reception desk.

Eventually, he was led through to another austere room that embodied all the uncomfortable precepts of the Sundowners: hot, still and unfurnished save for a raised platform with a single carpet for comfort. A small window did more harm than good. No attempt at temperature control—that would deviate from the 'natural'. At least he wouldn't have to sit on the floor. The knees were getting stiff these days.

Two lawmakers came into the room. He shook their hands, touched his heart, showed palms.

'I am Aaron,' said the older lawmaker. 'You requested me?'

Paperback said, 'Is it really true?'

He had to hear them say it.

'It has come upon us, as fate does,' intoned Aaron. And then, less formally: 'We meant to warn the river people earlier, but you understand, we have been preoccupied.' He stepped aside and gestured to the other, younger lawmaker. 'My colleague, Eyre, will be our witness.'

Paperback swallowed dismay. Instinct warned of a dangerous gulf between him and this pair. As a librarian he had always affected the air of a dishevelled scholar, hair flying every which way and a superfluous glamour to his dress. Today he wore a suit jacket with a sarong and some old cavalry boots. Perhaps he should have made a concession. The Sundowners seemed to have reverted to some austere core, swapping their usual clothes for some kind of cotton pajama, devotion shown by the ash striping their faces. Their severity cut right through Paperback's absent-minded disguise. It occurred to him now that everyone he'd seen today had shaved their heads down to the pale, naked scalp. He felt the seed of panic.

Begin with gifts.

'A small something for you.'

He unwrapped some silvery dried fish and set down a clay jar of preserved apple. Aaron smiled and leaned forward, only to catch himself. Adopting an erect formality, he adjusted his thick, ash-smeared glasses.

'Thank you,' Aaron said, 'but no.'

Did the younger one ever blink?

'Ah—sorry.' Paperback laughed. 'I forgot that you are now fasting. I just thought you might need every meal you could get under your belt for th—, th—, *the*—'

'For the *flames*,' said Aaron, and Paperback sensed a slight regret. The older man was the sympathetic one.

'It comes not a moment too soon,' said Eyre.

Paperback knew to approach the sacred with care.

'Ah, I see,' he said, 'How did you know it was time?'

The younger lawmaker smiled.

'The signs are clear to the pure of heart. That so many are surprised is itself a sign. Decadence causes blindness.'

Paperback nodded as if he understood.

'There isn't some special calendar, then?' *Don't attempt humour!* He looked closer at the man's face, unblemished beneath the cosmetic ash. 'You'd be too young to remember the last fire.'

The smile remained fixed and distant—but somehow evolved into disdain. Paperback tried to paste his hair down. The buffoon from downriver was not welcome today. Where was the patrician in him now? He was the eldest in the room. Yesterday the urchins had been so afraid of him, shouting orders and stomping.

He stood up and buttoned his jacket.

'I *must* ask you not to light this fire!'

'It's not up to us,' said Eyre.

'Well—it *is* though, isn't it? You are the government.'

'It is not up to the government.'

'Then who has the final say?'

'None of us have a hand in fate.'

Paperback's skin crawled cold.

'*Your* hand lights the fire!'

'Our sympathies,' interjected Aaron.

'But there is dry forest running all the way downriver to my place! How long do you think it will take for the fire to reach me?'

'The flames exist beyond law,' recited the older man, in order to impress the younger.

Paperback felt a sudden stab in his heart from the future. He turned to Aaron, searching for understanding.

'Do you know how long it has taken me to build? My whole life!'

'We are all subject equally,' said Eyre.

'I am not your subject.'

'All are subject to the flames.'

Paperback couldn't look at him. The youthful face was shining with sweat, the eyes without pity. There was no air in here. Paperback went to the small window.

'But you have a beautiful town. Your homes!'

'Those who survive will rebuild and improve.'

The older one had a heart in him. He came to stand by Paperback, to explain.

'Look there, do you see how the streets are full of refuse? We have outgrown the sewerage system. How we have lapsed! Our citizens compete with each other over nothing at all. They quarrel incessantly, they murder from desire. They enslave each other with debt.' He sighed. 'Things grow tangled with time— it's the nature of people. They become soft, they forget what life is for. There is only one clear path to make things simple.'

The heat was building in the room. Eyre shone from the dais. Aaron's oversized glasses made him seem harmless. Paperback had the impression that he somehow pitied the fool from downriver. The older man blinked behind his ash-smeared spectacles and said: 'You should feel some satisfaction that your fish traps will survive the flames.'

'But—your schools!'

'A building is not a school.'

The one called Eyre had tired of this discussion. 'We know that your weakness, *bookkeeper*, is to own books.' He seemed to see Paperback for the first time. 'You believe that this brings wisdom.'

Paperback had to defend himself.

'I own *worlds*.'

'Words on a page are not the thing itself. That's an illusion.'

'And yet I can go inside these books! I can visit many lives! I can know those worlds. Their people become as close as kin when I read their stories.'

'We have heard of your perversion for fiction.'

'What can your children do with all this endless rote learning of things they can't begin to comprehend?'

He hadn't meant to insult them, but time was short.

Aaron was still trying to get him to understand.

'You underestimate our way of learning. Our young may not understand what they memorise, but it lives inside them for the rest of their days. You visit a book. They *become* the book. What can you do except hunt for things in dead pages that the flames will eat in an instant? Our people have their entire lives to unravel the knowledge they swallow.'

Paperback narrowed his eyes.

'I am very careful what goes into my library—I have a system! The subjects cover every area of life…' In a last attempt, he searched his bag for a magazine. 'Here is one you might like: how to please a woman. Not interested?'

The older lawmaker seemed curious, but Eyre interrupted.

'You pretend to own these books, but they prevent you from moving freely. We spread learning through our entire population so that the green shoots will appear again from the ashes. We *eat* knowledge. Can you say the same?'

The building creaked under the sun. *Running out of time.*

'Could it be,' Paperback wondered, 'that you fear your people's faith is fading? I hear talk.'

Eyre didn't flinch. 'Could it be that you are afraid to lose what is owed you, bookie? Many of our people have gambled with you and lost. Soon all debts will be wiped clean.'

'Even abstraction is decadence to you fanatics—you think you can collapse ambiguity. My god! There've been suicides since your announcement.'

'It is all part of the process.'

'How many will have to die?'

Aaron seemed sad that he had failed to convince. He sighed.

'We are all fuel.'

'But it hasn't started,' Paperback cried. 'You don't have to light the fire!'

The younger lawmaker stood, walked to the door and opened it for Paperback to leave.

'It is *you* who fails to understand, stranger. The process is already under way. The fire began long before any of us were born.'

Paperback went out into streets that should have been a chaos of human preparation. But they were empty, save for a bitter wind that stirred the dust.

The urchins watched him, each grubby face a book that might never be read. He threw them the dirty magazine and they fought over it. Then he went to find some ethanol for his unsprung cart. The buggy didn't roll much faster than walking pace, but at least it preserved the body's energy. It took most of the afternoon to return home. Haze blotted the sun until it was a burning coin you could look right in the eye. There was more water downriver, the still brown pools connecting to make a single channel.

Would it be enough?

He should have been salvaging what he could from the garden, and certainly he should only be taking with him volumes of practical knowledge, the paper accumulation of science and human achievement. So why were only the most useless novels piled up waiting to embark?

Without pause, he loaded his rickety boat down to the waterline, praying there would be enough river to see him all the way. Hot wind filled the air with smoke now. When the sun hid its face a mob of grey kangas crashed out of the bush in a sinewy panic. And when he finally pushed off into the water, flames could be seen flickering through the trees.

You Think I Can't
Do Hard Things

Lucy Nelson

B's best scar was the white line across the width of her abdomen. The caesarean. Puckered pink edges. She wouldn't touch it. So I kissed it, put my lips on it. She sighed loudly when I did that.

The first of her two babies tore her perineum. The second gave her that scar and made her knees and ankles ridged with varicose veins. There was still a small blue knot behind her right knee. I kissed that too. She joked that her breasts became empty socks after breastfeeding. They hurt to touch for so long that she stopped thinking of them as anything but functional.

And those were just the baby scars. She had others. A hockey game. A hot skillet. A motorbike.

She touched my scars too. Across my palm: a puffy white slug from when I slipped in a rock pool. I was nineteen. I had been drinking beer in the sun for hours. On my hip: a raised disc left over from childhood chickenpox. Those are the only stories my body saw fit to document. I don't play sport. I don't ride motorbikes. I haven't had babies.

When she talked about her oldest child, twenty-two by then, a vertical crease appeared from her nose to her forehead, and her eyes clouded.

There was this book launch at her faculty building one night. Cheese plates and prosecco in plastic tumblers. I spent all night listening to stories about other people's children. I got lumped in corners with the other wives like hardened sugar—all so young it was difficult for me to picture them driving, let alone raising children. They took turns parroting the funny things toddlers say. Maybe because of my greying hair, they assumed I would find their stories adorable. I obliged. I nodded. I cooed. I looked around for B who spoke quietly with men in suit jackets. Neither smiling nor frowning.

She came to kiss me on my cheek, and we said good evening to her boss, the stern professor, and his wife, the architect. She was fifty-odd, closer to our vintage. I tried and failed to imagine her in bed with the stern professor. She seemed to cup her long, thin hands around an invisible basketball as she spoke. Soon talk turned to her hens.

'Fresh eggs every day,' she said. 'And if you walk up and down the fence line they follow you, making these inquiring little sounds. They're so lovely. I'm tempted to invite them inside to watch telly at night.' At this last revelation, the invisible basketball deflated to a golf ball and she cupped it to her sternum, as if to contain her hen-love.

B gave her tolerant smile. By then I knew the meaning of each particular twitch and tightening. I was always good at reading her face, ever since the impossible prize of new and reciprocal love had stunned us both back to life.

On those early Saturdays, we lay on the day bed in my sunroom. We floated inside something buoyant, protected. We circumnavigated the edges of each other's pasts, trying to feel the shapes in their entirety: *Do you still speak to him? Do you think she forgave you? How long did you feel broken? When did you stop feeling broken? How did you get so...* until we were too exhausted to talk. B always wanted to make something of the morning, when it came around again. I always wished she would stay in bed.

'I'm dying for chickens,' I told the professor's wife. It was true. There was an empty hutch in our yard. Waiting for them.

'Buy her some chickens!' the woman implored. She spoke to B as though she was a man in a 1960s sitcom, and I was the naive housewife. *You should bring this one for dinner! You've been keeping her from us!* I turned to B, who was collecting olive pips in her grimy napkin.

'I love this woman,' replied B. And then—as a performative aside—to me: 'I love you. Which is why I know you will never keep chickens.'

B, the professor and his wife all tittered. It sounded like a laugh track. I laughed too, but the implication stung. That I'm not a grown-up. Not capable. I park over the white lines. I fiddle too long with the latch on the gate. I can't connect the gas hose. I buy the wrong light bulbs.

One day a male colleague asked me very pointedly if I had kids. When I said no, he looked me up and down and said, 'You seem like the kind of person who would have kids. I don't know why. You just do.' He seemed to wait for me to explain myself, but I didn't.

'I know why,' B said hotly over dinner that same night while I recounted his words. 'You have a vagina.'

'It's my hips,' I said, still upset from his roaming eyes. 'My stupid child-bearing hips.'

B elicited the opposite reaction in her colleagues. She encountered surprise when she brought up the topic of her own two children.

'I guess I don't look very maternal,' she said.

B is analytical and perceptive, which people can read as cold. Not me. I read it as wise. Once you see her that way, you can imagine her giving young people exactly the kind of instruction they need to tie a shoelace, end a dysfunctional romance or decide on a gap year. And then the evidence of her warmth blooms again and again.

I often thought of B raising her two kids. How naturally she would have taken to the demands of parenting. I used to love imagining it, used to wish we'd met earlier so I could have seen her as a young mum. But lately, the image had started to pang; the lines between her strengths and my deficits were too quickly and easily drawn. She had always been deft, nimble; a calm problem-solver, a multitasker. I had always been slow, clumsy; a one-thing-at-a-timer.

I used to think I could show her how good it feels to slow down, but her momentum was too strong. She had to keep moving. My stillness made no difference. There was no time for it. She set a pace and I dragged my feet. Did she pretend to enjoy it at first—my stillness? Did the thought of slowing down ever appeal at all?

B made a show of holding my hand and said, maybe for the entertainment of the stern professor: 'How long has that empty hen house been sitting in the yard, my love?'

I hated this show she was happy to star in. I shot her a look: a censored, in-public version of something private. It hurt to conceal it. It burned.

She ignored me. She looked at her stern supervisor and said, 'Tell her about the time one of your chooks got sick and you had to bury it in the garden.'

'Okay,' I conceded, holding my palms up, indulging everyone. Performing the role of The Girl Who Can't Get Her Hands Dirty. 'Don't tell me. I've heard enough. Let's not get chickens.'

As soon as we were in the car, my scarf felt like a garrotte. I unwound it urgently, giving off an exhausted groan and slumping into the passenger seat. I fiddled with B's phone, trying to connect it to the forgetful speaker. Every time we turned off the engine, the stereo seemed to wipe its memory clean. And every time we got back in, it had to rediscover us, taking several goes to reconnect.

'What?' She watched me jab at her phone's screen with my index finger.

'I'm so sick of stories about people's children. None of them are funny.'

She frowned at the stereo display as it sought a connection. I rattled off the anecdotes I'd spent the evening nodding along to.

'Some kid refused to leave home without his favourite spoon. Another one accused Santa of being homophobic—'

'Okay, *that* one is funny,' she interrupted.

'—One is going through a clingy phase. Another bit a boy at kindy. And then they laugh and say: *Why would anyone have children?* And they touch me on the arm, as though they really believe that! As though they didn't *choose* this! As though they really think they've got the raw end of the deal!'

'What deal?' B reached for the phone, and I gave it to her, admitting defeat. She tick-ticked through the settings with two agile thumbs.

'You know,' I said. 'The sacrifices they make so they can know how it feels to have their hearts walk around outside their body. Isn't that what it's like? I know I can take things the wrong way when I'm tired. But I'm so sick of them telling me they're more exhausted than I could possibly understand.'

We both went quiet for a minute while B concentrated. A robotic voice said: 'Disconnected, ready to pair.'

'It's a different kind of exhaustion when you have kids,' B said. 'That's all.'

I slouched at the very sound of the word *exhaustion*. Earlier that morning I'd caught the 6.09 train to the gallery. I tried to get there earlier than the incessant wave of calls and questions, which always started rolling in at eight. I proofed an exhibition catalogue. I read twenty-four job applications. I answered eighty-five emails. My eyes hurt from my screen. I sat in meetings until six. I caught the tram to the book launch. I looked for B's thin frame, her slight stoop in the crowded foyer, I listened to stories about other people's children.

'That's not what they're getting at,' I said. 'It's like people without kids aren't *allowed* to be tired.'

She frowned up at the rear-view mirror.

'I don't think that's what they mean.' She thumbed the car display, choosing a playlist. She liked to listen to classical when she drove. She hit play and went to turn the engine over but stopped when she saw me rigid in my seat. She knew I needed her to listen with her whole body when I was like that. She slowed down. She waited for me.

'I don't like being patronised by these people,' I said, and turned my face away. The car park was neat, rectangular, with trees spaced more evenly than is natural. We'd parked right beside one. I fixed my gaze on the swirled knot in its slender trunk. I remembered painting our toenails the same shade of fire-engine red while we sat naked in banana lounges in my backyard. I remembered us laughing at the imprints the plastic slats left on each of our backsides.

'Well, you don't have to come next time,' she said.

'I didn't mean that.'

She went again to turn on the ignition but stopped and exhaled. This is how it went: she gathered the strength she needed to be the bigger person and make peace. She cupped a hand on my knee, jiggled it, and said, 'Who patronised you? Tell me their names and I'll have them beaten up.'

I turned back to face her.

'You did.'

'I'm sorry?' She gave me her best confused face.

'I have a job too.'

'I know you do.' She withdrew her hand.

'You're not the only one with deadlines.'

I was determined to chip away at the surface of her calm until a crack appeared, so I could squeeze through it and reach around for evidence of something loose, untethered. Some shred of irrational thinking to make us even.

She gripped the wheel. Ten and two. Eager to move, to be purposeful.

'I know you have deadlines.'

'It's not about *deadlines*, B. You think I can't do things!' It erupted from me.

She gave me a pained smile. 'That's not true.' Her tendency is to placate, to find reason in the face of tension.

'You think I can't *do* anything.'

She could have said that no, of course she doesn't think that, but we both knew that would only make me madder.

'I backpacked around India alone! I run a gallery! I'm an *adult.*' I felt like a child insisting they were nine-and-a-*half.* Wanting to prove I was competent despite appearances.

'Oh Jesus, the India thing again.' There. A crack. She took the key out of the ignition altogether. 'This is your stuff! *You* think you can't do things. It's your youngest-child complex.'

'Oh, for fucks' sake.'

She shrugged.

'I was serious about the chickens!'

'I know you were *serious* about the chickens,' she said. 'And you were *serious* about taking an upholstery class and fixing the armchair that's been sitting on the back deck for a year. And you're *serious* about going back to school and finishing your thesis. You *say* you're going to do things.'

My chest filled with something dark and branching. My eyes darted back and forth across the width of the windscreen. I was looking for something. In my mind, I saw the ugly parts of me she was finally naming and watched as they formed a horrible beast she couldn't possibly love. It was satisfying. Moments after solving a riddle, the earliest clues appear suddenly obvious. I was diving into the ugliness then, dredging for the things I'd always sensed were ripening there.

We sat in silence. I felt her grow smaller, recoiling from her words. I relished her regret. My own guilt is a vapour: clinging, faint, permanent. The car park around us was emptying out. A streetlight buzzed on and the shadows in her face sharpened.

Some part of me was already climbing out of the car and catching a tram to Ruth's place. She's always got wine in the fridge. I could curl up in her bed like a dog, I thought. But before I could decide to reach down for my bag, B was driving us home and we were moving at her pace again.

On the drive home I looked at my own reflection in the passenger window. Slack-jawed. Shell-shocked. I gripped my thighs just to feel something soft.

As soon as we were inside, I brewed a pot of coffee and went straight to my desk. She watched me from the doorframe of the study, leaning. I typed quickly. I reached for a light switch. I opened drawers to look for things I didn't need. For once, she was still and I was rapid. But both of us were only trying it on for size.

I barely needed to ask B to move out. Her understanding was swift. Of course it was. In the week that followed, she seemed to construct each new cardboard box before the last one was taped closed.

She's not gone from the house completely. I still fill the jug she sometimes used as a vase and test the soil of the indoor plants with my finger like she taught me. But unruliness returns. A stack of books curves precariously on the arm of my leather couch. A new painting has been leaning against the wall beside the front door for three weeks. I am in no rush to hang it. I am considering hanging it. I have adopted three chickens. I am considering a dog.

At B's place I know everything will be in order. Even her artwork is educational: antique, sepia-tinted maps showing how the world used to be before cracks appeared to form new oceans; botanical illustrations with the Latin names printed beneath each flower. After a few months, I hear from a friend that she started dating someone new.

Exactly as the professor's wife predicted, I come to love the company of hens. They follow me along the fence line as I rake and weed, appraising my methods. They gather at my feet in curious congregation, as though eager for news. I go out in the morning to scatter feed and touch the warm eggs, smeared with gunk. At night I change the water and wonder what they are saying to one another.

One night I come home late from the gallery and turn the yard light on. I freeze on the spot, my heart thudding in my ears. Instantly I recognise one of the hens. It's Tushy, named for her fluffy grey rump. She is a long stretch of fluff, feathers, sinew and dark red blood. Her head and neck are missing. Still frozen, my eyes search the yard and pause at another mess of feathers and blood. Jolie, my favourite. The third old girl, Viv, is nowhere. She must have panicked and run while the other two were being attacked. But she can't have gone far. I start to walk very slowly into the depths of the yard, sensor lights flickering on and illuminating blood and feathers as I go.

The night feels airless. I am trapped inside it, alone with something sinister. Alone with blood. I feel that something might come and take my head and neck too. I can't find Viv. I go inside to call B before my better judgment can overrule.

I stay inside until she arrives. I can't be alone with the mess again. I stay still in the kitchen; I can hear my own blood roaring. Then I move into the hall, waiting for the sound of her engine. When B opens the front door, she holds me straight away.

'I must have left the hutch open,' I confess through tears. 'You were right. I can't keep chickens.'

'Rubbish,' she says, and rocks me. 'It was just a mistake.'

I feel her jumper dampening beneath my cheek.

She holds my shoulders and smiles into my eyes. Her gaze is like a doctor's pen torch, but instead of looking for the way my eyes react to light, she is looking for a crack in my self-loathing. 'There we go,' she says, as I smile a bit. She makes me a cup of tea and tells me to stay inside and drink it.

She was always deft in the kitchen. She'd have three pots on the boil and still make you a cup of coffee. She is used to doing many things for many people. She doesn't know how to take her time. Even in the shower—which I treat as a luxurious escape—she would be efficient and systematic. Hair first, so she could soap up the rest of her while the conditioner sits. She wouldn't shave anything because shaving serves no purpose. This game of function and result would only stop when she lay down to sleep. Even then, she would go from conscious to unconscious with impressive speed.

I try to stay inside, but I can't bear that she is out there alone. I haven't heard her make a noise since she went into the backyard. Surely, she's disturbed and disgusted, but she is trying to keep it together for my sake. I start to worry and go out to the back step. She is fine. Nothing has come to take her head and neck. She is wearing rubber gloves, raking the bloodied straw into piles and stuffing it into garbage bags, already bulging from the plump, motionless bodies of Tushy and Jolie.

'Thank you,' I squeak.

'You poor thing. What a horrible fright.'

I've always found her kindness soothing, but tonight I have no right to it. It is only on loan for the evening. It sinks faster than I can touch it. I step closer and see that her grey jumper is flecked with bits of blood and slime.

I crane my head and think I hear a low croaking. I look at B. She hears it too. We follow the sound into the far corner of the yard.

There is Viv beside a fence post. Whatever attacked the others had a go at her too, but it has left her alive. There is a slice down the length of her neck, and she is quivering in a sticky pool of her own dark blood.

I turn to look at B whose hand is over her mouth. 'Oh God.' She looks the way I must have looked when I first discovered the carnage. She just stands there, staring.

I march to the shed and take the long-handled shovel from its hook on the wall. 'Don't look,' I say to B, who does as I say.

I know the quickest, most painless way is to sever the head. With my eyes pinned on Viv's neck, I raise the shovel in the air and swing it down. The croaking stops. It's done.

In the shower, I scrub my whole body clean. When I emerge in a towel, dizzy from the steam, B is in the kitchen, wearing one of my clean T-shirts and offering me another. I picture her going home to someone else in my clothes.

She hugs me and says, 'That was kind, the way you ended things.'

There is a wound in the webbing of my thumb. I'd gripped the shovel so hard, determined to get the horrible business done in one go. I wish it were something likelier to scar. I wish my body would see fit to make all of this a more permanent event.

Illegal Alien

Jumaana Abdu

The illegal alien claimed he was from the past. He claimed many convenient and impossible things. That he was an Australian, that he had studied biology and anthropology at a prestigious university, that he had been hired by NASA, that he had been sent on a lightspeed mission to survey a healthier world exhibiting signs of intelligent life. And that he had returned, as directed, to his home, the planet Earth, in the interim of which had eclipsed a few hundred Gregorian years.

'I envy you,' Dr Gillam said, eyeing the brief projecting from his holoband. The UV-filter windows in his office cast the room in a purple hue, which made his skin look green. 'But I know why they chose you to go see him. It's the "nun effect". Patients see a hijab and suddenly they're confessing.' He was my senior, so I laughed, but only half-heartedly. This incurred a sceptical eye. 'Or maybe it's because you're a woman and they figured out a sure-fire way to get any red-blooded male who's been alone for centuries to prove that he's a human being.'

'I suppose it has nothing to do with my PhD,' I offered politely. He became distracted by a sun sore on his hand which, after he scratched it, began to flake and bleed. I reminded him, 'My paper on the psychiatry of displacement?' The information did not appear to register. I surrendered and moved on. 'Genetically, I'm not sure it will be so easy to prove whether he is or isn't human—'

Dr Gillam huffed and began scratching another sun sore on his eyelid.

'The vessel he arrived in is too advanced to have come from the century he claims,' he said. 'And his story is fantastical regardless. When you hear hooves, think horses, not zebras. It doesn't take a genius to do this job. It'll be like telling the difference between being alive and being dead.'

I had nothing to say to him. I couldn't imagine what it was like to be so uninterested in the definition of 'living'. And what was so inconceivable about zebras? But I wanted the meeting to end, so I suggested, 'Well, since he supposedly looks like us, acts like us, there is the possibility that he really is from Earth, returning—'

'Let me make it perfectly clear,' said Dr Gillam, reaching for a tissue to dab on his ear. He was riddled with sores—typical for a man of his generation who grew up before it was mandated to wear SPF 90. He lowered his voice and leaned forwards. 'There is no historical record of this "man". Besides, it is against international law to send men on lightspeed missions through outer space. And with all the conspiracies running riot that the rich and powerful are buying one-way tickets to a cooler planet… It is not your role to make accusations. Forget possibilities. Anything that is not from this planet is not a human being.'

A few things had prompted me to accept the assignment which government officials had described with disclaimers such as 'risk of exposure to lethal biological matter' and 'indeterminable consequences on the mind' and 'first in the history of humankind'. I was ambitious, and to have a patient whose diagnosis lay on the scale of time, space and humanity seemed enough to justify an academic tenure. But, mainly, I was spending all day as second-in-command to Dr Gillam at the Defence Hospital, all evening as last-in-command to my parents for as long as I continued to be so blatantly unmarried, and every second of every day wanting anything to happen to me—even something 'lethal' and 'indeterminable'—because I was so, so *bored*.

I'd read what limited information I had been provided. In the brief, there were no pictures, and he was referred to by number only. I'd seen the viral footage circulating on social networks of a small aircraft almost burning up on re-entry into the atmosphere over the Great Dividing Range. It was a lonely image. That loneliness made me inclined to believe he was a human being.

So I found it bizarre and disconcerting how difficult they made it for me to carry out my pre-approved visit. Security made a grand ordeal of external sterilisation and signing non-disclosure agreements and waiving a multitude of my human rights and putting me through checkpoint after checkpoint.

Finally, after waiting hours for transport, they blindfolded me for the duration of the dronejetter flight before kicking me out into a muggy climate. A rough voice projecting from my holoband instructed me to uncover my eyes. I was at the doorstep of a small demountable with a doormat that read *WELCOME*.

'Am I here?'

But when I threw a glance over my shoulder, I found there was no one else around. The dronejetter was a freckle in the sky. The heat was painful, which meant I was under an ozone gap. I appeared to be on a tropical island large enough to accommodate a tiny community. The demountable before me had been electrobarbed off from all others nearby, and the transparent shimmer of the shield stretched farcically high. In the distance, over a vast strait, I thought I saw a haze of land that was my country.

I turned back to the door and raised my hand. Then I froze. The door seemed suddenly to be a trap; I had the impression of a large, hungry animal sitting behind it.

In the end, I knocked.

After a minute, I heard shuffling noises and then the door opened to reveal—this was my first thought—a man.

His posture was stooped. He seemed ground away. But when he glanced at me, almost with disinterest, a thunderclap transformed his expression. His eyes widened and his mouth opened, and the wind knocked out of his chest sent tears springing to his eyes. It took me a moment to understand the look was one not of pain or terror but of the most basic and surprising joy. He dropped his head and placed his hand over his chest.

'Assalāmu ʿalaikum,' he greeted.

Automatically, I replied, 'Wa ʿalaikum assalām.' I knew then that Dr Gillam had been right about why they had sent me.

The man—the being—recovered himself and gestured for me to follow him inside. I commenced my examination of his surroundings. The interior of the demountable was a single room with an ensuite. It was bare and neutral-toned save for a few pillows on the ground, which I supposed were his bedding. I watched him hastily rearrange them to create a sitting place. No desk, no books, no writing utensils. The only light came from a skylight in the ceiling. There was a flap at ground level on the back wall; I assumed it was for animals until I saw the remnants of a meal in a tray beneath it. If he was indeed a man, this was a prison. If he was not, it was a cage.

'Please,' my patient said, redirecting my attention to the pillow he had placed nearest to the corner. I sat cross-legged and he mimicked me, leaning against the adjacent wall.

'Are you a doctor?' he asked.

'Yes.'

And then he was quiet and still.

There was no way around it; he looked like a man. He was wearing a white jumpsuit with white socks. His face was long and kind, and his hair was the colour of tree resin, downy and floating around his head in some places as though under the sway of balloon static. Even his beard was fine and soft, and his eyes were flecked with gold. His skin was dark but remarkably clear of sunspots, which made me self-conscious about my own. I couldn't tell his ethnicity. I considered the possibility that racial mixings had been different a few centuries ago. Only there was something in his wide brow and his clear expression that made him seem unusually noble, that made him seem like a man from outer space.

'I wish I could offer you something to eat or drink,' he said, gesturing to the empty enclosure.

'I'm fine,' I assured him. We were both breathing quickly, both blinking too much and both sitting upright with a pole of adrenaline bolted to our spines. I began unpacking my briefcase. 'Thank you for agreeing to speak with me.'

'Agreeing?' His gaze landed on the inside of my briefcase. I felt him cataloguing my equipment, attempting to guess the use of everything as a biologist or an anthropologist would. Then he laughed in disbelief. 'I've been asking to speak to a doctor. Nobody told me you were coming.'

This was news to me, but I felt it was best not to disclose as much. My holoband was recording everything we were saying and, I suspected, broadcasting it live to Defence.

'I haven't seen a human face in almost a year,' he went on as I set up my kit. His accent was strange, although that didn't mean much. 'I've been travelling for so long. And since I arrived, the guards have worn armour over their faces so all I can see is my own reflection. But it's useful, since they won't give me a mirror.' He looked at me with curiosity. 'Shouldn't you be wearing a surgical mask?'

The suggestion amused me, and so I surrendered to my urge to look back into his face.

'Surgical masks don't do anything,' I said. Then I opened my mouth wide so he could make out the shimmer of the breathable biofilm sealing the space between my lips. His wonderment was intense. His pupils dilated.

'Incredible,' he breathed, tilting his head. 'Is it organic?'

I nodded. 'From some kind of extremophilic lichen.'

He laughed again, and the sound was like mellow chimes, light and resonant. All the time I was thinking, *This has to be a human being.* He caught me watching.

'What's your name?' he asked quickly, as if it was his last chance to grab a foothold.

'I'm not allowed to tell you.' I raised the holoband on my wrist so he could see the blinking light. Whether or not he knew what it was, he understood. For a moment, his eyes glittered with resentment.

'And if I tell you mine?'

'You will be punished,' I told him flatly.

And then we were serious. I rearranged my pillow so I was sitting directly opposite him. I wanted things to be formal. I needed the authority of my position.

'Do you know why I'm here?' I asked.

'I know why I asked for a doctor. I thought, of all people, a doctor might help me.'

'I'm here to determine your humanity.' He must have known it already, but his eyes dropped in shame, which was probably the point. 'Did you ask for a Muslim doctor?'

'No.' He gave me a sympathetic look. 'They sent you to test me.'

He was right, of course, and he probably also knew, as I did, that no amount of questioning could allow me to judge whether or not he was telling the truth about his beliefs, because to be a Muslim was not a password but a state of the heart, and I could very well auscultate what his heart sounded like but only God could know what it was saying. They had not just sent me to 'test' him but to taunt him. There was the threat of dignity in his face.

He slapped his hands on his knees and stood up with a grunt, spreading his arms out wide like an anatomical drawing.

'Go ahead,' he said. I stood to match him, and for all the assessment in my eyes, there was assessment in his. He joked darkly, 'Am I allowed to consent?'

I wished he were less intelligent. It would have made it easier to assert the doctor-patient dynamic. We both knew he was being violated, not only his flesh but his privacy, since I was reporting back to strange, faceless men every confession of his body, down to the script in the nuclei of his cells.

I examined him in silence for the rest of the afternoon. It was not a distancing silence. It was the companionable concentration of two scientists in the field. Occasionally, he interrupted it to inquire about the mechanism of a certain device, and often this was followed by an admiring comment on the advance of technology. He was particularly taken by the holoband, which I used to auscultate his heart sounds by pressing my wrist against his sternum. The band projected sounds of his heart valves bursting open and slamming shut, the iambic pentameter testifying he was alive. He wasn't bewildered, only impressed.

'Very handy,' he said.

I tested his reflexes, listened to his lungs, shone a light into his eyes, and then made him lie down so I could perform a rudimentary survey of his viscera with an ultrasound. I even looked at his fingerprints under a nanoscope: *Human.*

When it came time to take his blood, he became suddenly unsure.

'What do you need it for?' he asked.

'DNA.'

'Right, of course,' he said, but he didn't relax. 'And how soon will you know the result?'

'Almost immediately.'

He took a long breath in and out. It was the first time since meeting him that I reminded myself there was a chance he might be alien. I wondered what calculations he was making. Ultimately, he sat down and rolled up his sleeve. I was aware of his body heat as I ran my thumb over the crook of his elbow. His brachial pulse was bounding, and then I came across his median cubital vein. I wiped it with an alcohol swab. His skin shone.

'Sharp scratch,' I said.

He held his breath. And then the needle was in. When dark fluid came flowing into my syringe, we both relaxed audibly.

'*Sharp scratch*,' he echoed. 'My doctor used to say the same thing.'

I extracted several syringes and he submitted without protest. With some trepidation, he watched me connect the first syringe to my gene assay machine.

'You seem nervous,' I said under my breath. I risked a glance at him. 'Isn't this what you wanted?'

'I'm not sure now… I'm sure I was a human being when I arrived,' he said. 'Under these conditions, I don't see how I could still be. It seems counterproductive to their goal.'

'And what do you think their "goal" is?' I humoured him, bandaging his puncture wound.

'You said I would be punished if I said the wrong thing. But I'm being punished already,' he said. 'I'm being punished for being a stranger. Like the sleepers of Ephesus, or whatever name you know them by. They sought refuge from persecution in a cave, and when they awoke from sleep they thought they had been gone no more than a day. They went down to the townspeople, not realising they had slept through many years, and the strangeness of their clothes and their money made the people afraid. If the past is a foreign country, then what does that make me? Do you know that quote?'

I shook my head.

'We used to say it in my time. "The past is a foreign country." Maybe the future is an enemy state. And the present is what? A hung jury? A gridlocked congress?'

I laughed because I thought he was wonderful.

'What's a congress?' I asked.

A wistfulness came over his face. 'I feel like you're younger than me,' he said. 'But I think we're the same age.'

The gene assay machine dinged. We startled and turned to it. The screen read: *HUMAN*.

We both stared, willing it to mean something conclusive. The truth was, not even a genetic verdict could keep me from rationalising his humanity away. Off the top of my head, there was panspermia—the theory that our species existed in other galaxies, originating from the same biological seed as human beings on Earth. It would mean that, genetically, he could pass for human, maybe even technically *was* human, but it wouldn't matter. What mattered was how he had come here, and whether he was allowed to stay. He seemed to have come to that understanding before I did—the DNA result gave him no relief.

'I'm dying,' he said.

I looked to him for signs of malaise, but his cheeks were flushed with health and his eyes were bright.

'I'm dying in here. I don't have any books, not even a pen. I haven't spoken with another person in…I don't know how long. Even all this politeness is cruel. I miss people, I miss animals and trees. I'm not allowed to step beyond the front door or a microchip in my shoulder will shock me. They won't even let me have a map of Australia. They won't even admit Australia is a country.'

'It's not,' I told him. 'We don't call it that anymore. We gave it a better name.'

'What is it?'

'I'm not allowed to say.'

He looked into my face for a long time, and in the abyss between what we wanted from each other and what we could give I felt all the distance between two alien beings. My honesty was up against two opposing demands: his longing to be pronounced a man, and the government's preference that he was not. The existence of lightspeed technology was a Pandora's box; if this traveller was human, it would confirm widespread suspicions that those who could afford it were buying a way out of the heat. It would spell global riots and political disaster.

But then, if he was *alien*, to accept him, to 'open the doors' in such a way to the entire cosmos… The consequences could be cataclysmic.

The sun was setting; darkness seeped into the enclosure. I felt dampened by the shadow. I stood and took a turn about the room and he followed suit. I noticed his footfall was completely soundless. I only heard the swishing fabric of his clothes. The windows were beyond reach so it was impossible to see outside. The air conditioner groaned, washing stale air around the room. I kept circling, trying to think.

After a while, I stopped and turned to face him. He came to such an immediate reciprocal halt that I had the sense he was mirroring me. I examined him. He examined me back. Was I alien to him—I, who was from a future country? The only unearthly thing about him was his hair. Even the inertia of coming to a standstill had been enough to send it floating out of place. Maybe his body had forgotten about gravity. The thought made me so light-headed I had to return to my makeshift seat. He watched me in the dark, unmoved. After a moment, he lowered himself to the ground beside me.

'Most nights, I have a dream that someone has finally been allowed to come see me,' he said in a hushed voice. 'Every time I hear them knock, I sprint to open the door, but it's locked. I try to break it down, I throw my whole body against it, and I can hear their voice on the other side, but I can't make out what they're saying. I scream, "You have keys! Use your keys!" And just as I hear them put keys into the lock, a gunshot goes off, and they die.'

His breath was quiet and measured. I thought of his alveoli, the chemistry of gas exchange.

'We don't have guns anymore,' I whispered.

'Good. But what about my dream?'

'I think it means you're lonely.' I thought it meant his loneliness was being weaponised. And then a sudden awareness of our alliance alarmed me, along with embarrassment at the possibility that I was being duped. 'The planet is burning,' I said to confront him. 'I wouldn't have come back. I don't know why anyone would.'

'I'm sure you do,' he told me. 'It's human nature.'

Sadness landed a blow to my chest. 'How could you do it?' I asked, buckling. 'How could you leave, knowing the probability that you would die, or never see your friends and family again?'

'Haven't you risked all that by coming to see me? Given the promise of what you might find, what would you have done in my place?'

In the unlit room, with the halo of delicate hair floating around his face, I felt like we were in an expanding darkness that stretched on and on, infinitely. It seemed fitting that this room was his home.

'Do you have dreams about travelling to other planets?' I asked quietly, even though I knew the microphone in my holoband would pick up everything regardless. A fleck of gold twinkled in his eye like an evening star. He turned his face to the skylight.

'Of course,' he said casually. 'I dream all sorts of things. One place, in particular: bright and temperate, flush with greenery, sweet-tasting rivers, leaves larger than a man, winged creatures, animals with tails, mountains that erupt with fire, and people—all sorts of people, people that look exactly like you or me, so much that you might even think they were human beings. I dream of this planet as often as I would if it were my home.'

'What is it named?'

'They don't name places the way we do here. In their language, they call it "the world". I dream of going to the world and being welcomed. I dream they introduce me to a man they call "the archivist". He sits with me and is as eager to learn from me as he is to teach me. I learn about his god, he learns about mine, and I feel our beliefs are the same. We swap languages, prayers, food, history, science, literature, clothes, names. These are his people's units of exchange.'

'It sounds beautiful,' I said.

'Yes.'

I turned to him. His eyes were clear, open.

'Do you ever dream that you make a deal with the archivist, and he returns to Earth in your place?' I asked.

A small huff of air escaped him. It was hard to make out his expression in the dark. It could have been humour or disappointment. But fear, unmistakable, rang through his next question: 'What will happen to me if they don't believe I am a man?'

'I don't know. You could be expelled.'

A beat of silence passed. He sat up and turned on the lamp. I stayed seated, watching him. I felt emptied. The muscles in his jaw tightened and would not unclench.

'How?' he asked rigidly. His face seemed lit with a solar glow. His eyes burned. 'I mean, physically, literally—how? Even if I really am alien like they say, even if I survive the journey back, everyone I know on that planet will have died by the time I arrive. It would be the worst kind of exile. I would be as alien to those people as I am to you now. I could spend eternity being expelled back and forth.' His body began to tremble like iron rods under immense pressure. 'Is this what it means to be human? To treat each other this way? Should I be cruel, too, so you'll be forced to accept me as one of your own?'

In a sudden movement, he seized me by the shoulders, so I was forced to look at the desperation in his face. I tried pushing him off, but his strength was extraordinary. The gentleness in him had been replaced by fury and pain.

'What do I have to do,' he begged, 'to prove I can be cruel? I'll do anything! I'm scared what I might do!'

'Calm yourself!' I cried, and for the first time I was afraid. I eventually managed to throw him off and flee to the opposite side of the room, wondering why the dronejetter hadn't come to evacuate me already. I looked around for a weapon, but the room was empty—there was nothing to kill another person with, or even yourself.

My assailant was still kneeling on the ground. He seemed dazed. He looked down at his hands and then up at me, uncomprehending.

'I'm so sorry,' he said. 'I've never been violent in my life.'

I ran my hands over my face and let out a long breath. I couldn't blame him. It was too much. I was exhausted. There seemed to be nowhere left for us to go, no way for us to help each other. Slowly, I approached him and knelt by his side.

'Pray with me before I go,' I said.

He looked to me in surprise.

'Why?'

'Because whether or not you're a man...' I sighed. I had lost the ability to care what my holoband would hear. 'I believe that you have a soul.'

When he saw I was sincere, something speared him, and he looked at me with terrible longing. And when he moved again, I thought this time he would really attack me, but all he did was come close enough to whisper in my ear his true name.

'Oh, no,' I said. It was over. I knew it was over even before I heard the blades of the dronejetter descending in an emergency landing just outside the front door. With desperation, with love—not romantic love, it was more than that—I burst with a sob: 'Oh, God, why did you tell me? I told you, you're not allowed to tell me your name! They won't let me back here anymore! You'll be reassigned! Why did you say it? Was it so important for me to know?'

'Yes,' he said, full of pity. 'Thank you. It was important. I believe it has saved me.'

Someone bashed in the front door, but he didn't seem to notice. The smile on his face was otherworldly.

After weeks of quarantine, I was back in Dr Gillam's purple office. My holoband had been taken into government custody, replaced with a permanent comms plate under my skin.

I sat staring at the sun spots on my hands while Dr Gillam lectured me. The traveller's hands had been dark, smooth, unblemished. It was illegal to mention him to my parents, but I would have kept him secret anyway. I still had a bruise where he had touched me.

Now Dr Gillam informed me that after stalling immense pressure to address viral footage of the vessel arriving, Defence was releasing confirmation of the traveller's existence today, as well as the verdict that he was an alien being. This was Dr Gillam's official impression, arrived at after a two-minute telehealth consultation.

'What will we do to him?' I asked.

Dr Gillam gave a noncommittal shrug.

'We've got to figure out where he should go. It could take years. It could take forever.'

Nothing he was saying registered in my mind. I felt like someone had swapped my life out for a replica in the short time I'd been away. I didn't recognise ordinary things. When people spoke to me, I couldn't understand what they were saying. I looked back at my own hands, at the roping of my veins. *Sharp scratch*, I thought. How would he know that unless he was a human being?

Dr Gillam clicked his fingers irritably in front of my face, and it made a patch of his skin flake off onto the desk. He smelt like flesh rotting in the sun. Before he could berate me, someone screamed down on the street. Dr Gillam delayed his reproachment to investigate at his window, then I heard him invoke a deity. The terror in his voice brought me back from a flatline.

'Th-th-there's *more,*' he exhaled.

I joined him across the room. In the distance, in the cold sky, like falling stars, were tiny objects blazing through the atmosphere.

Dr Gillam fell apart. He started raving, racing to the phone to roar down the receiver. On the streets, more and more people joined in on the hysteria.

I can't say what I was feeling. The bruise on my arm became hot. I knew I should have also been afraid for my country, for the world, but I was thinking only of the people inside those vessels hurtling down to the Earth. I thought about how alone they were. I thought about how long they had been waiting to see us. I thought of them imagining our welcome, coming to us with so much hope that their ships were burning.

It's Possible

Paige Clark

After a wet, cold summer and a wet, cold winter, there was another summer the same, followed by a winter that was dry and warm. Even though this August could have passed for October, nobody seemed to mind. There were picnics, pool parties and people wearing linen. Everyone talked about the premature spring as if it were a present, as if the yellowing grass, crisp underfoot, was not a sign of what might happen come January.

Bella knew that the smell of spring was actually the smell of worms. Now, as she ambled to the park with her young son, she scrutinised the revellers she saw on the way, with their bare arms and exposed legs, tanning in the winter sun. But she had to look away from those who swam boldly at the unheated public baths. It was simply too much.

Bella wore her coat—a Kathmandu puffer—to wish the weather away. She knew that if she changed her actions, she could change the future. There had been enough evidence of this for her to trust that this was true. She had, for example, kept her entire family alive by always knocking on wood, three precise knocks—though not necessarily *on wood*. The good things that had happened to her were because she had never broken a mirror, and she, in every instance, had thrown spilt salt over both shoulders. The bad things were clearly a result of her carelessness. She was an ethnic; she took old wives' tales to heart.

Even better if the superstitions were backed up by a scientific study. When she was pregnant, she'd read that women who had heartburn gave birth to babies with hair and women without heartburn gave birth to babies with no hair. Bella was desperate for her baby to be born with hair. Most babies without hair—white babies—looked like a version of Mr Clean and not much cuter. True, most babies like her— Chinese babies—had hair. Her unborn son was only a quarter Chinese though, and early on she'd had no heartburn to speak of. So she ate Shin noodles, salads with large chunks of raw onion, obscene quantities of spaghetti bolognese. She drank pint-sized glasses of fresh-squeezed orange juice with pulp. In week thirty-three, she had a single pang of discomfort behind her breastbone.

After Bella's first twelve hours of labour augmented by Pitocin, an obstetrician came to check her dilation.

'Does he have hair?'

'You're six centimetres dilated.'

'Can you see it?'

'The dilation?'

'The hair.'

'I have only delivered one Asian baby where I did not see the baby's hair. I saw a foot,' the obstetrician replied. 'An undiagnosed breech birth.'

'Did the baby have hair?'

'It did.'

One emergency C-section later, she held her son in her arms and stroked his wet, black hair. He doesn't have as much hair though, she thought, as I did. That was eighteen months ago. Her son had been born in the first cool January. Back then, she had been grateful for the mild weather. She'd been in what others referred to as the baby bubble.

In her short time as the boy's mother, Bella's mind had been populated with every single nursery rhyme and simple song ever sung in the Western world. There was one for every occasion: getting into the pram, leaving the park, driving in the car. For once in her life, she cared to know little besides this: how to please another person. In pregnancy, her mind had been a sieve, but now it was a colander—retaining only what she needed to know, like how he preferred his toast cut (small squares), what temperature he liked his bath drawn (38.5 degrees) and what flavour of liquid paracetamol he would tolerate (orange). Once upon a time, she had known things that mattered to other people. Once upon a time, she had gone to an office job and typed things into a computer.

They reached the park and entered the playground through a security fence. Bella handed her son a loose doggy bag from her pocket so he could pretend to be a dog owner by picking up fistfuls of tanbark. Solely by observation, he'd mastered the inverted-bag technique. Bella still struggled with this technique herself. Last week, rushing to retrieve her dog's faeces while the toddler demanded a rousing performance of 'B-I-N-G-O', she'd smeared hot poo across the palm of her hand.

The playground was fully fenced in and situated across from the designated dog area, which wasn't. The park was situated on a ten-lane dual carriageway, and before her son was born Bella wouldn't take her dog to this park because of a fear he might run across the road. After her son was born, however, she took her dog to this park because it was the closest to her home. Sometimes she and her son went alone to the playground. Other times, they took the dog to the dog section. On rare occasions, Bella would let the dog into the playground. But only when there were no other kids there. Under no circumstances would Bella let the dog play at the dog park alone while she and her son were over at the playground.

Her son clutched a bagful of tanbark and walked to the bin. Bella sat on a swing and watched him trot back and forth, stooping down every so often to pick up a handful of tanbark or rocks or rubbish. He'd always been partial to chomping on, well, everything. Bella often googled when this would end. The answer was soon or never. She was a nail-biter, after all. Best to be on high alert. Most days, she left the park with a pocket full of hazards: half-empty soy sauce fish, dirt-encrusted bottle caps, triangle remains of cellophane bags.

Her son's poop-scooping was interrupted by the click of the security gate. A white family entered the park—a mother pushing a baby in a pram accompanied by a small girl on a balance bike.

'Bubba!' her son said.

At first, Bella thought he was talking about the baby. Then she realised he was talking about the girl. He had a habit of calling a child older than he was a baby.

The mother parked herself on a bench and sat rocking the pram back and forth with her foot. The daughter sat next to her. The mother handed her an almond croissant, which the girl held up to her mouth but did not eat.

Bella's son, who was an extrovert like his father, approached the family. He waved from the wrist, his hand cupped like a pageant contestant. Then he said, 'Hello, croissant.'

The little girl did not reply. Perhaps because he was talking to the pastry and not to her. The croissant also did not reply. The girl's mother peered into her phone as if it held a formula for how to parent.

Bella's phone knew more than she did, too. She did not have the motherly instincts that women mentioned to her before and after her son was born. Her gut simply told her that something terrible had happened or would happen soon. Before she even served her son's breakfast, he choked on an unsquashed blueberry. He ate dirt and contracted botulism instantly. He stopped breathing every time she placed him in his cot. Thankfully, her intuition had so far had a strike rate of zero. And the rest of the information she did need on parenting was waiting to be discovered on Reddit. Or on one of the four Due Date Facebook groups she had joined. Or a quick search away on the Mumsnet forum.

'Hello, bubba. Hello, croissant.'

'Let these people eat in peace, honey.' Bella led her son away towards the slide.

At some point in time, the little white girl stopped holding the croissant and started playing near the swings. She'd brought with her a white baby doll. At first, she put the doll in the baby swing and pushed the doll up into the air as high as she could. Next she twisted the seat round and round and round until the swing's chains were tightly coiled like a snake enveloping prey. Then she let go. The doll spun rapidly until it flew off the swing. The mother continued to stare at her phone. Bella and her son watched the girl in amazement. In her previous life, Bella had never shown any interest in physics, but since her son had been born she was fascinated by the world and the way it worked. She'd marvelled at dinosaurs and diggers, at automobiles and aeroplanes.

'Wheeeee,' Bella said as the doll spun around again in the swing.

'Wheeeee,' said her son.

The girl said nothing but smiled widely. She stamped her light-up runners in the tanbark. Bella's son stamped in reply. He was wearing gumboots. Bella had been optimistic there would be rain.

'Again,' said her son.

The girl did not reply but placed the baby doll in the swing again and began twisting, twisting.

Bored of the game, Bella peered across at the dog portion of the park and saw her nemesis, the owner of a schnauzer who had once gotten in a blue with her chihuahua cross Pomeranian. This schnauzer got into many disagreements. He did not like other dogs. This was a common trait in dogs. It was a common trait in people, too. Her son, as if intuiting where she did not want him to go, walked to the fence that separated the playground from the dog section. The schnauzer waltzed over, as did the owner, who had a lit cigarette in one hand and a retractable lead in the other. Bad owners always reeled their dogs in like they were fish.

Whenever Bella saw the schnauzer at the dog park, she would tell him, 'Get, you get.' But since her dog was not there today, she could not in good conscience tell the schnauzer to leave. She looked at the other dogs at the park; she knew them all. They could all hold their own against a schnauzer.

Bella returned her attention to the playground. The girl was now crouched down beside the pram, pawing at an unopened bag of lollies in the basket.

'If you touch that packet again, you can kiss your croissant goodbye!' the mother said.

The girl dragged her light-up shoes back and forth in the dirt. The mother returned to her phone. Her foot still jiggled the pram even though, as far as Bella could tell, the baby had made no sound. Strange how the mother never peered in to see if they were still breathing.

Her son followed a line of ants up the playground stairs and across the wobbly bridge. He'd recently graduated to crossing the wobbly bridge without her hand, an accomplishment that made her proud and plaintive in equal measure. He poked at an ant with a stick. The ant became a smear.

'Ant, ant?' he asked, and even though Bella knew he had not meant to be cruel, she couldn't help but remember the summers she had spent as a child with a magnifying glass pointed at the pavement. She knew what it was like for a body to burn to death.

A dog barked, alerting Bella to the arrival of a greyhound in a black skivvy with a silver-studded collar. The owner let the dog off a rope slip-lead and it began to run in circles. The schnauzer paced back and forth in a puddle at the foot of the drinking fountain, paws shrinking in size like a dog after a bath.

A man in his sixties or seventies—the owner of the greyhound—now entered the gated playground. He was weedy and white and wearing exercise gloves. Since birth, her son'd had a fondness for white men like that of his paternal lineage. She wondered when she'd have to burst *that* bubble.

'Man,' her son said. She had never taught him the word.

'Person,' she said.

'I'm here to use the monkey bars,' the man said. 'Cheaper than the gym.'

'Ooh-ooh-ahh-ahh,' her son replied. 'Monkey.'

Bella forced an expression that resembled a smile and scooted closer to her son. The man did not seem like a predator, which was at once reassuring and unnerving. But what did a predator seem like? Surely a predator would not announce himself so boldly or have a greyhound that was dressed up so divinely.

Bella looked to the other mother for guidance, but she did not look up. Bella did not trust herself or her assertions about a situation. She was prone to act on her paranoia. She had asked her husband once if he trusted his father to change their son's nappy.

'That man raised me,' her husband had replied.

Even this hadn't been enough for her. She quizzed her sister-in-law, poking and prodding her with questions as if some unknown family trauma would come spilling out. None did. It's still possible, though, she thought to herself.

Upon the greyhound owner's arrival, the little girl had left the safety of the spot of ground next to the pram to veer at him. It was fast becoming clear that he was no more threatening to the little girl than her own son was; in fact, he was even less threatening. The girl waved and watched as the man did pull-ups on the bars and then push-ups. He was noisy and vocal. He could have been an actor performing exercise on a stage.

The girl ventured back to her mother. She pointed her finger towards the man.

'My turn. Monkey bars.'

Bella waited for the mother to look up and catch sight of the man working out, but when she did, Bella was relieved that the woman seemed unfazed by what she saw huffing and puffing on the jungle gym.

'Sure,' the mother said. 'Fine.'

The little girl ran back towards the bars—still occupied— and past them to the slide. She climbed onto the bottom and sat there staring at the man working out. She wore the same delirious grin as she had while spinning the baby doll round and round in the swing. It was then that Bella noticed the girl had wet her pants. The pee soaked through her leggings in the shape of a horseshoe.

For a minute, Bella stopped sensing what was happening there in the park and started remembering something about her own childhood. At first, it was just the memory of a sensation, of that warm wetness. Then the recollection that it had been on a family trip to Disneyland. She must have been seven. She had no spare clothes and so her mother bought her Little Mermaid pyjamas from the shop in Fantasyland. Her mother made her wear those pyjamas to school every day for a week to remind Bella of her error.

It was not Bella's job to be a mother to this child. It was not her responsibility. Children wet their pants. They were ignored by their mothers. They were denied soft lollies and scolded and even spanked!

She felt it was better to pay attention to her son, who was currently poking a stick in the tanbark. He was using the stick to drum on the sheet metal stairs that led to the slide. Her son was singing Old MacDonald to himself. He was singing 'E-I-E-I-O-O-O'. He was calling out: 'Dog! Dogs! Doggy! Baby dog!' He was approaching the man and blowing him a kiss. The man seemed to look past her son and across to the park to where the greyhound sprinted, playing, perhaps.

'Beautiful,' the man said to Bella. 'Beautiful boy.'

'Where the fuck is my dog?' someone at the dog park shouted.

Bella paused. She knew intuitively her nemesis could not recall her dog. It's possible the owner had been training the dog. But it's possible she had not. When Bella's dog had gotten in a fight with the schnauzer, the two dogs had engaged in a standoff, both baring their teeth, not moving. Since the owner of the schnauzer could not recall her dog, the woman had been forced to walk over to him and kick him with her boot until he backed down. Bella had not been able to intervene because she was nursing her baby on a park bench. Not the right time or place for it, she knew.

So when she now heard someone screaming 'Here, boy, here,' she hoped it was not the owner of the schnauzer. But it was. The dog was standing at the edge of the dog park about to step onto the road. The other day Bella had counted five cement mixers that drove by. It was a game she and her son played. Her son spotted countless motorbikes and buses and ambulances. They saw a dump truck and an auto carrier. Before her son was born, she had only noticed how busy the road was. She had never noticed what the road was busy with.

The other mother recalled her little girl. She was pleading with her, begging for her to get on the balance bike. She either did not notice the soaked pants or did not care. The baby woke up and began to wail.

It was too hot for the goddamned puffer.

Bella unzipped her coat, took it off. The other mother cajoled her daughter onto the bike with the promise of sweet television, and then they were gone. From a distance, Bella couldn't tell if the baby was still crying or if she was simply still hearing it.

The man left through the security gate, returned to the dog section and put his greyhound on the roped lead. That racing dog was regal in his turtleneck and jewellery. Perhaps he had not been playing after all. Perhaps greyhounds only ran for a reason.

The schnauzer stood still on the kerb between the park and the carriageway. The dog did not turn back to see what was no longer behind it but looked forward to see where it could not go. The owner ran towards the schnauzer, the retractable lead limp in her outstretched hand. Bella did not watch as the owner latched the dog's collar to the clip. She turned her attention to watch which way the man and the greyhound had gone; it was not the same direction as her own home.

'Up, up, Mumma,' her son said. She picked him up and pressed his flushed cheek to hers. His small hands were toasty. She shivered even though it was unlike any winter she'd ever known.

'I've got you,' she said.

'Mumma got you,' her son replied.

She did, but for how long?

Despite everything, other people couldn't see what was coming or didn't care.

Spur

Alice Bishop

The job request comes through during the quiet hours, as calls for total write-offs often do: reports of crumpled tin, glittering glass and sand-softened bitumen. It's early September; sock weather still. Jules D'Angelo sleep-squints towards the lilac screen of his charging phone, the glow highlighting the deepening lines of his face. Outside, the moon's honeyed and high; hours, yet, before morning.

Private number, the screen reads.

A boobook owl calls, breaking the shuffling silence—its *mopoke mopoke* a steady punctuation of the night. It'll soon be warm enough for termite flies. One swirling mass of beige, the insects will mill about the security light—out to multiply before shedding papery wings. Thousands will wriggle through daylight-savings dinners all over the valley: drowning in Fanta cans, over blue-black grills, semidetached wings plastered to barbecue grease.

Private number, the phone again glows.

Jules' skin gives off a bready scent—stale, vinegary, warm—as he reaches across his bedside table, cluttered with blue BIC lighters, pocket change, crumpled track receipts. Twisted down around his legs, his sheets—navy cotton blend, cheap—are laced with Omo snow, with engine grease.

'Yarra Glen Towing,' he answers.

A small pause on the other end. Then the drone of hushed conversation continues in the background: distant voices, the pad of keyboards, the white-noise whir of other urgent late-night calls. The murmurings make Jules think of the low hum and click of hospital machinery: coagulating tissue, restoring rhythm to blue-pink. He thinks of saline drips, white sheets and the honeycomb holes of broken bone.

A low voice surfaces.

'Yeah, got it mate. Thanks.'

There's a haze to it still, not yet for him.

'Hello?' Jules prompts.

'Nah…can't get on to the family yet…'

The ding of a microwave. A plastic-kettle click.

'Yarra Glen Towing here… Hello?' Jules, a little louder now, repeats.

'Mate, mate, sorry,' the voice on the line answers, quiet still but now clearly directed at him. There's a clarity. A new frequency. Homing in.

'Senior Officer Deng Chol here…VicPol and all that…but you know it though, the old drill.'

'Bud,' Jules acknowledges, picturing Deng's round face, and then the invoice he'll be able to work up: night rates he'll be able to request. He goes through the list he's started saving for: repairs for the broken water pump, the worn-through brake pads of the driveway sedan. The holiday in Aotearoa he'd once planned.

'Come see the glaciers before they go,' his now silver-haired sister Cate had said. 'The glow worms? Or come see me, the kids, aye bro?'

'You been asleep? Sorry...' Deng continues. Jules pictures his KeepCup, its glass fogged. A white desk covered in folders. He knows the cool fluorescent lights of the valley station, the grid posters of all those faded faces—years disappeared.

'Yeah, pretty asleep, mate,' Jules continues, pulling the sheets over the gentle curve of his stomach and wiping his forehead with a small, callused hand. He clears the lingering taste of red wine, of chip salt, with a swig from a crumpled water bottle by the bed. 'What've you lot got for me, then?'

A lengthy yelp travels down from the ridge. A fox, Jules thinks, *pad-jaw trapped and calling out for her kits.* He thinks about the whole smiling families of them he once passed near the old Healesville highway—strung up by their tails along glinting silver fence. About the kelpie he once had as a kid, its soft folded ears flapping, eyes determined, as it nipped at the wheels of passing things—its chirpy yip of excitement, no time to shift before the slip.

'Clean-up...four cylinder...' The officer's voice interrupts his trailing thoughts. 'Total write-off...fatality, unfortunately. Needs to go to the Southbank shed.'

Jules looks across the room, the shadows of thrown clothes appearing as his eyes adjust. The shape of his loyal lavender heeler glows grey as she stays sleeping, breathing heavily as usual from her favourite hessian rug. There's the outline of his clothes rack, too: six different versions of the same check shirt; a suit jacket still in its drycleaner bag; his father's old motorbike jacket, scratched up, wide-shouldered and worn.

The hum of the old fridge turns over down the hall. Inside it: Pura, on-sale mince, coleslaw, crumb-streaked margarine.

'Black Spur, mate. Up near the corner of Monda Road.' On the line, Deng's voice, hushed and deep, continues. 'Let me shoot you a pin?'

Jules pulls on an old woollen jumper: alpacas marching around his chest. Once neatly knitted, they're now warped: necks much longer than their knotted legs. He pulls on his stretched boots, then jeans—flecked with paint and faded at the knees. *Least it's not a track vest, a tight helmet strap around my chin*, he thinks.

Grabbing his keys from the coffee table, Jules calculates the time he had his last drink. He then considers the other possible demerit points, as listed in the Accident Towing Services Regulations 2019. He runs through the checklist: *Points taken if driver of rostered tow truck fails to: take reasonable steps to attend accident scene within thirty minutes; ensure removal of debris and glass from road accident scene; display legislated warning lights.*

Too easy, he thinks.

There's a damp to the drive along the ridge, gristle fern carpeting the edges of bitumen. Old-growth mountain ash and moss-covered rock borders each of the hairpin turns. *Danger zone*, signs read. *Drive carefully*. Some of these signs are pockmarked by tiny bullets—a spattering of dark holes through wind-curled tin. Jules breathes in, regrips the wheel, and pushes in the clutch as he lowers the gear. The big engine transitions down, before he accelerates back through the turn.

Larger tree ferns, lush and prehistoric-looking, shadow the curve. *2.2 kilometres to your destination*, the cradled phone glows. Jules shifts his sleepy weight in the seat as he passes another VicRoads sign with large changeable numbers. *336 motorcycle accidents this year.* A dull ache blooms up his healed left leg, silver pins clawing bone. He remembers the ambulance at Flemington Racecourse, before his career change. A wet feeling. That earthy, metallic smell. The bright light of people rushing to secure his neck. His breathes in deeply, remembering the early morning smell of horse—earthy, sweet.

Part regret, part relief.

Trees thicken closer to the summit and undergrowth bends. Road ridged and ready for an upgrade, the truck tremors with the unstable ground; main winch and safety chains jangling from the tray behind Jules's head. *200 metres to destination*, the navigator screen now reads, red pin dotting the winding line.

100 metres.

50 metres.

You have arrived.

Jules recalls the feeling of being boxed in: mud hitting his goggles from the thoroughbreds out front. The rhythm of hoof on turf, of a horse's football-sized heart beneath him, his own pulse in his neck. He remembers the blur of the bright white barrier, the race caller's drone: *And they're all under pressure at the midway point now…the strong gelding from Geelong out front by a length and a half…and a few at the back of the pack, not to disregard, still going strong.*

You have arrived, the computerised voice repeats.

Two traffic-control sticks glow orange up ahead. The wands gently move in deliberate semicircles: like festival lights directing the tow truck to the scene. Jules shifts the truck down again, begins pulling up onto the slim shoulder of bitumen. Stunned by the headlights at first, a grey-muzzled wallaby thumps softly off into the dark ahead.

Jules can't quite make out the face of the person holding the amber lights as he brakes gently, lowering the truck into first gear. The big vehicle softly groans to a halt. Unclipping his seatbelt, he then leans over to put on the hazard lights. His safety vest and gloves. The heater continues to hum as he makes sure to note the time, 4.16am, on his device.

A beeping sound fills the truck cabin as he opens the door.

'Mornin', mate,' the emergency worker in mandarin overalls says.

A sooty owl calls through the night.

'Morning,' Jules nods back, noting the lack of tyre marks on the road.

'This one's just glided off,' the tall woman continues, the residue of a dark lipstick still staining her lips. 'No brakes—nothing.' Her face is unreadable as she gestures towards flattened fern. 'Other side of the embankment there. Ploughed straight into one of the hundred-year-olds.'

Jules looks across without seeing the wreck—just the flattened path of the car—then up. The old, giant mountain ash gently swaying overhead, the half-filled moon, a sprinkle of stars. The night's quiet again, apart from the distant hiss of the engine, the shuffle of something furred, nocturnal and small in the understory. A tiny bat soon flits by, after a single termite fly.

'Okay, let's see how we'll pull this one out,' says Jules, walking towards the road's edge.

The woman nods again. She reaches for her phone while turning back towards the row of witches hats already set up. 'Yeah, clean-up's finally here,' she says quietly into her device. 'Ambulance, cops, long gone…a fatality unfortunately, yeah… we'll wrap up here soon.'

The smell of leaking engine fluid wafts off the cream Commodore, its seats covered in pink. The glovebox has been crushed, its contents—sesame bar wrappers, a spare phone charger and sunscreen—pressed into one. Through moonlight Jules can make out the hole cut-out where the roof once was, more flattened fern, moss and scrub around the driver's side door, pried clean off.

A single missed synthetic slide.

The smoked twang of airbag sulphur.

Climate Action Now, the yellow bumper sticker reads.

The pulsing glow of hazard lights up again, followed by the shuffle of workboots making their way through the tangled understory towards him. A swaying torch follows.

'A real mess, hey.' The tall woman's gentle voice reaches him.

Jules' body has made the connection before the rest of him—the muscles of his short legs wobbling with adrenaline, with cortisol. It's an effort to keep his knees locked, his thick ankles from buckling and the feeling in his feet from suddenly leaving.

He remembers the scented vanilla tree he'd tied to the rear-view mirror, how it smelt of laneway jasmine, of McDonald's soft serve and the special spray his aunt Linda used for the fridge. He remembers leaving the small Yarra Glen house feeling as close as he'd ever felt to being parentally proud.

'A good first car. Steady. Reliable,' he'd said, and his old friend's family—all three of them—had smiled back at him. Having once ridden beside Jules at Yarra Glen track meets, Cheryl had been grateful to get his help for her daughter's first vehicle. 'Sure, I'll pull through,' he'd winked. 'Something solid. Something durable. Bulletproof.'

Another sooty owl call.

'You think you'll pull this up easy enough?'

Jules tries to answer, sound snagged by his closing throat. He swallows, the flavours of chip salt, red wine and now the bright tang of bile filling his mouth. He closes his eyes.

The woman lowers her torch. Another shuffle and shift through scrub.

'Yeah,' Jules answers quietly, his stomach folding. He steadies himself by reaching out for the moist trunk of a tree fern, the texture a forgotten shag rug—left out in the weather too long.

'Sorry,' he says. 'So sorry,' he says again as the sharp smell of his warm vomit suddenly mixes with the rich forest: moss, must, mulch. The roadside hazard lights are now those from the Flemington ambulance again.

'Steady,' a gentle but unfamiliar voice is saying. 'It's all right mate…help is here.'

'You win some, you lose some,' Cheryl had said quietly when she visited him in hospital after the fall. The lines of her face had bunched in a familiar smile as her eldest daughter had stood beside her, clutching a crumpled box of Roses chocolates and a warm bottle of white wine.

The smell of bile rises again. The torch flickers, threatening to go out. Jules straightens up, silver pins again clinging.

'Okay then.' He nods. 'Let's get this done.'

Dinner Scene

Erin Gough

I was waiting in the front room with Skips on my lap when Sean Evergreen rang the doorbell. I'd been there for fifteen minutes in a chair beside the curtained window that looked out onto the path. I'd watched him jump out of his mum's run-down Mercedes, walk up the steps and disappear onto the porch. Seconds later the electric chime filled our hallway.

The dog pricked his ears but didn't move. I put a hand on his black silky head, feeling the heat of it, running my fingers along the ridges of his skull. Skips didn't mind this. You could do anything with him. He'd been in our family since I was small. A part of me wanted to just sit there with him, my fingers rising and falling to the rhythm of his breath.

I heard my mother from the other end of the house.

'Caroline, the doorbell.'

I picked up the dog and settled him on the carpet, folding his arthritic legs into his body. I straightened my skirt, walked into the hallway without answering my mother and opened the door.

'Hello,' Sean said, and smiled.

He'd dressed up. Beneath his blazer, he was wearing a turtleneck jumper, which I didn't much like. He looked like he'd raided his father's wardrobe. It was the same outfit he'd been wearing at the college dorm party a month ago—the night we'd been introduced. He leaned in, placed one hand lightly on my waist and kissed me on the lips.

'I'll just let my mother know I'm going,' I said when the kiss was finished. I thought about my mother, who still hadn't met him yet. 'Want to come in?'

Sean shrugged. *Your call*, said his shoulders.

'Is that him out there?' my mother asked when I entered our living room. She was sitting on the couch reading the *Telegraph*. 'Howard Slashes Immigration,' was the headline beneath a photo of the Prime Minister and Pauline Hanson. Reading the paper was unusual behaviour for her on a Saturday night. Typically, when my father was stuck at work, she'd spend the time cooking meals to freeze for the week ahead.

'We're running late,' I said. 'I'll see you around eleven.'

My mother put down the paper and looked at me. 'Please say hello to Linda Aitken from me. You'll remember to do that for me, won't you, Caroline?'

'Yes, Mum.'

Her eyes narrowed. 'Your skirt's crumpled.'

'It's dinner,' I said, making my irritation clear. 'We'll be sitting down.'

My mother's expression changed from critical to something else. 'Well, at least change your lipstick. That colour clashes with your top. Here.' She went over to her handbag on the kitchen bench and returned with a lipstick and a tissue. I waited as she wiped off my lipstick and applied the new one.

'There. That's a bit better.' She took a step back and gazed into my face, which irritated me further. She'd been gazing at me this way a lot lately. I didn't know why, or whether she ever found what she was looking for.

Jess Aitken, host of the dinner party, lived in a wealthy suburb a half-hour drive away. Camphor laurels lined the footpaths and large houses hid behind thick hedges or fences of iron or stone. Out here, you could walk down the street without a clue about what was going on inside people's homes: arguments and polite conversation rang the same note of silence behind the yawning lawns.

We'd been friends since our first year in high school. It was Jess who had introduced me to Sean: she lived on campus at the women's college, even though the university was a short commute from her parents' house. She knew him from their modern history tutorial. 'He's good-looking—not to the same standard as Richard, of course.' Richard was her boyfriend—a former Grammar boy who was studying medical science in the hopes of following in the footsteps of his anaesthetist father. 'But Sean's sweet. He's studying arts commerce. Not everyone can get the marks for law school,' she'd added, poking me in the ribs. 'You'll like him. He's a bit shy and a bit of a study head. Like you.'

It was not overwhelming praise for either of us, but then Jess wasn't one for compliments. The only exception to this rule was when she spoke about her older brother Oliver.

Despite Jess's assessment, I wasn't entirely convinced that Sean was shy. He'd kissed me first, which tended to disprove her theory, although it was only a first move in the technical sense—a drunken embrace at the end of the night after three hours of my conscientious flirting. He *was* quiet though—she was right about that. When we stopped at the Aitkens' house, he locked the car and we made our way up the long winding path without speaking. I didn't mind it. We reached the heavy timber door with its stained-glass panelling—a waratah rendered in swirls of red and green. I lifted the brass ring knocker and struck it a few times against the plate. Sean fiddled with his jacket, pulling the cuffs down over his wrists and tugging at the hem with his long pale fingers. The door opened and Mrs Aitken stood on the step, beaming at us.

'Caroline,' she said in her intense way, clutching my hand. She wore a woollen skirt with a cashmere jumper—I'd seen the same one featured in one of my mother's magazines. 'How lovely to see you.'

Of Jess's friends, I was Mrs Aitken's favourite: she'd told me this more than once. I knew it had to do with my high marks at school; she considered me a good influence. Because of this, I felt a vague sense of unease, as if I were somehow responsible for Jess. I feared that at some point the Aitkens would remember that my father was just a pool salesman from Botany, and that my mother spent her days in a demountable answering his phones, and cut me off. (Of course, Mrs Aitken herself didn't need to work. Her husband was an ex-barrister turned Supreme Court judge.) The fact they hadn't banished me yet made me feel peculiarly beholden to Jess's mother.

'Hi, Mrs Aitken,' I said cheerily. I introduced Sean.

Mrs Aitken turned her beam upon him with full flattering force and pressed his hand into her own.

'Sean. A real pleasure. Please, go through. The others are out the back.'

Standing on the porch with Mrs Aitken's warm gaze upon us, I recalled how the last time my mother had been here she'd barraged Jess's mother with praise about her hydrangeas while

Mrs Aitken smiled politely, her usual ebullience absent. I decided not to mention my mother to her.

I led Sean by the hand down the hallway with its wide floorboards and salmon-coloured walls. Sean's hand was moist, his grip loose, but it felt good. I followed the sound of voices to the sitting room.

Jess and Richard sat on the couch, her hand flopped across his knee. As we came in, Richard straightened, his soft brown eyes following our progress. He wore a cable-knit jumper with tailored pants and brogues. One of his thin arms stretched across the cushion behind Jess, which she leant against delicately so as not to mess the hair that rose from her ears to a grand pile high at the back of her head. Jess was always doing things to her hair. She liked to try out dyes the way others tried on clothes. Alanis Morissette one week, Baby Spice the next. This week's shade of blonde emitted an almost nuclear glow. I could practically hear the crackle and hum of it from across the room.

Opposite the picture-perfect couple, facing away from the door, Angela Elardo leaned over the coffee table scraping soft cheese onto a water cracker. Angela was in my torts class and was beautiful, although it took a while to notice this fact. Jess had told me more than once how plain and boring she thought Angela was. She was not beautiful in a flashy way. She wore neat, well-made clothes in muted colours. Her voice was quiet and low. Her jewellery, while expensive, was understated—a pair of pearl drop earrings, a thin gold bracelet, a ring with a single diamond. Then you looked at her properly—at her green eyes, glowing skin and straight white teeth—and it jolted you.

I'd only spoken to Angela a handful of times and was still slightly dazzled whenever I saw her. Tonight she'd made no great effort; a simple linen dress and ballet flats, her hair in a chignon bun. But it was the sight of her, not Jess with her radiant hair and new silk top and black heels as shiny as a detailed limousine, that made me look down at my crumpled skirt and try to smooth it. She was laughing at something Jess's brother Oliver was saying. Oliver was also Angela's boyfriend. He was talking loudly and had his hand on the base of Angela's spine. Something that Jess and Richard couldn't see was how he kept stretching two fingers to stroke Angela further down as he told whatever story he was telling.

Richard caught my eye from across the room and smiled his friendly, crooked smile. Oliver turned around, his hand sliding cleanly from Angela's back.

'Caro!'

Angela kissed my cheek.

'This is Sean,' I said brightly.

'The famous Sean,' said Oliver, and pointed at me. 'This one won't shut up about you, I hear.'

The comment made me blush, with its implication that Jess and I spent our hours together talking of nothing else. The truth was that I'd barely said a word to Jess about Sean. It was something we'd argued about, in fact. Jess measured friendship in confidences. In the six months she and Richard had been going out she'd told me about their relationship in a lot more detail than I suspected Richard would have been comfortable with ('He stroked my hair and *cried*,' Jess reported, incredulous, after they'd first had sex). Now she expected me to return the favour. But the most Sean and I had done was kiss and rub against each other on his bed, fully clothed, while Portishead played on CD. It hadn't lasted long because his parents had come home. At one point, after I'd spent some time kissing his neck, I looked up and saw that his eyes were wide and staring at the ceiling. I didn't know what it meant, but it certainly wasn't something to tell Jess.

'We've met before, actually,' said Sean.

Oliver looked confused.

'You and me?'

'Sean went to school with my brother, remember?' said Angela.

I saw a muscle twitch in Oliver's cheek. Then he showed his teeth.

'Friends with Chris, are you? Then let me get you a drink.'

'Well, that's everyone now,' Jess said, standing up. 'We may as well move to the table.'

'Phoebe's not coming?' Richard sounded surprised, although I already knew.

'I didn't invite her,' said Jess bluntly. 'There's not enough room.' She gestured towards the table with a game-show model's flourish, her hair quivering brightly.

At the Aitkens' table, I sat with my chair a little further out than the others and watched people talk. I had a keen and sudden sense of being a spectator in my own life. Lately, I'd been feeling this more often, especially when I was with Jess. With so many new ideas and people around her since we'd started university, it was an effort to simply keep afloat. Tonight I felt watchful but distant, sluggish to react.

Jess's father, who appeared from one of the house's wings, had seated himself at the head of the table. The chair at the other end was reserved for Mrs Aitken, who was still preparing food. This was how it was whenever Jess had friends around—somehow other people always ended up doing the work. Not her father, though—instead the judge poured himself a generous glass of wine and asked us what clubs we had joined.

He spoke in a loud voice, partly because of the racket Oliver was making in the kitchen: we could hear him grunting as he tore through roast beef with an electric knife.

In his days at university, Mr Aitken (or 'Your Honour', as Jess liked to call him) told us, he'd been heavily involved in something called the Gaius Gracchus Society. 'They threw the best toga parties on campus,' he declared with a straight face.

I didn't want to imagine Jess's father in a toga. He was a sweaty man with a thick beard that Jess would stroke facetiously when she wanted something from him, usually money.

'There's a trick to togas, isn't there?' Richard said pleasantly. 'You're supposed to be able to fold them in a way so that they stay on without safety pins.'

'You're thinking of kimonos, Richard,' Jess said, patting her balloon of hair.

Richard looked thoughtful.

'I don't think kimonos ever need safety pins.'

'I'm sure it's kimonos,' insisted Jess.

The judge laughed.

'I can't believe we're still talking about this. Does anyone care, besides Richard?'

Richard flushed before laughing good-naturedly. I thought about our friend Phoebe, who hadn't been invited to dinner. Her mother was Japanese.

'Phoebe would know,' I said without thinking.

Jess stared at me. 'Phoebe isn't here,' she said coolly, and turned pointedly to my boyfriend. 'What about *you*, Sean? You've lived in Japan.'

Sean, who'd been watching Angela bring the first of the plates in, looked up.

'I have, yes.'

Angela set down one plate of beef and potatoes in front of me, and another in front of Jess. She put serving spoons beside the vegetables. Sean leaned forward to help her. Watching him do this, I tried to remember if I'd known he was a friend of Angela's brother. Was Chris the school friend he often talked about? I'd sometimes wondered about Angela's family: where they lived, what their house was like. I knew that she came from money. Her grandfather had migrated to Australia and made a fortune in the cotton industry.

I could hear Mrs Aitken in the kitchen, opening and closing cupboards. Oliver was still cutting the meat. For each new slice came the sound of him revving the knife and forcing it through flesh until it rutted against the chopping board.

'You've lived in Japan?' Richard asked Sean. 'Why were you there?'

'A student exchange,' said Sean.

'Tell us what it was like,' Jess demanded.

Sean glanced at me. Jess's bossiness was something we'd recently bonded over. I rolled my eyes in an exaggerated way and smiled. The lids of his eyes went heavy the way they did before he gave one of his rare grins; I felt a sudden rush of affection. He cleared his throat.

'Um, different from what I'd been used to. Scary at first, but exciting as well.'

'Which island were you on?' asked Richard.

'Hokkaido. In Sapporo.'

'I love that beer!' boomed Oliver from the kitchen.

'We're not talking about beer,' Jess yelled back.

'I was living near the university. With a family whose dad was a professor there. An amazing guy. He was...' Sean paused. 'He was killed during my stay, actually. On a visit to Tokyo. In the terrorist attack.'

The room went quiet.

'That's horrible,' murmured Angela.

'What terrorist attack?' asked Jess grumpily, as if we'd personally conspired to keep her in the dark about it.

'A group of religious fanatics released poisonous gas onto the subway,' Sean explained in a patient voice.

'Speaking of beer,' Oliver said, coming through the doorway with another plate of beef and potatoes. 'I have to tell you guys about what happened at the college bar on Thursday night.' He leaned over me to slide the meal in front of Sean. Bloody juice skittered over the porcelain.

'Sean was just telling us about Japan,' said Angela in a low voice.

Oliver waved her objection away.

'Believe me, this one's going to blow you out of the water.'

Angela looked like she was about to say something else, but instead she slid wordlessly into her chair. Oliver then gave an account of a drinking game that had ended with three college boys up the jacaranda tree in the university quad, naked.

'What I don't understand,' said Jess when he'd finished, serving herself some vegetables with one hand while the other one held up her hair, 'is what happened to their clothes.'

As Oliver repeated the relevant part of the story, Mrs Aitken came in from the kitchen, lit the candles on the mantelpiece and sat down. As soon as she picked up her cutlery, everyone began to eat. I reached for my fork half-heartedly, waiting for someone to draw the conversation back to Sean's story, but nobody did.

'Sean, you look like you could use some more wine,' said Jess's father.

Sean nodded, his jaw clenched. The judge leaned over and filled his glass.

'Oliver, this beef is *beautifully* cooked,' Mrs Aitken beamed from the other end of the table. 'Haven't I got a talented son?' The question was directed at the room.

'We all know he's marvellous, Mum,' Jess said, fiddling with a bobby pin that had come loose above her right ear. Oliver winked at her, and she grinned.

'The broccoli's delicious,' said Sean, looking at Angela.

'Oh, Angela always does very nice vegetables. It's her Italian blood.' Mr Aitken gave Angela a sultry look.

'Really, it's cooked to perfection, Oliver,' said Mrs Aitken, as if no one had said anything about Angela's broccoli.

This exchange made me think again of Phoebe. Earlier that week, while we were finishing our sandwiches on the Science Lawn, I'd mentioned Jess's dinner party.

'I'm not invited,' Phoebe told me. 'I must be out of favour.' She bounced her sneakers against the grass. 'Which is fine. I've never liked going to their place,' she added. She wrenched a handful of clover from the lawn. 'How their mother puts Jess and Oliver on pedestals. They can do no wrong. Nobody's good enough. Not even Richard, and Richard's great—and just as wealthy as they are.'

I was interested that Phoebe had noticed this habit of Mrs Aitken. It was so different to the way my mother spoke about me. My mother was far more likely to point out—both to old friends and complete strangers—a stain on my shirt than to say anything nice. Surely Mrs Aitken's approach was preferable.

'This dinner party. It's because I'm not in a couple,' concluded Phoebe.

I stared at her hazel eyes and dimpled cheeks, and wondered how anyone wouldn't want her around.

'That can't be it,' I said.

'Well, that's what's changed. Now you're with Sean it throws everything out. I'd just be dangling at the end of the table.' She waved her arms in the air and pulled a face, making me laugh.

I found Richard on my way back from the bathroom after the main course. He was in a shadowy part of the garden by the door that led out from the kitchen, with a beer.

He finished his mouthful and smiled. 'Getting some air.'

Further out a row of gums stood dark and still beyond the porch light's patchy glow. Behind them was a pebblecrete pool that my mother, who knew pools better than anyone (my father excepted, of course), often admired at high volume. At this time of night, you couldn't see it, but you knew it was there from the faint but distinctly acrid waft of chlorine.

'Having fun?' Richard asked.

I told him I was.

'You're probably wishing Phoebe was here.' He cocked his head.

I gave a noncommittal shrug.

Richard lifted the bottle to his mouth and emptied it. All the while his eyes were on me. 'You two have become close. Making Jess a bit jealous, I think.' He sounded apologetic.

I idly patted the trimmed hedge of lilly pillies that pressed against the back windows, although my mind was whirring. It hadn't occurred to me. Jess and I had a history that went back to when we were kids. If anything, in our tight trio Phoebe was always on the outer.

Although there *had* been one occasion when I'd visited Phoebe's place without Jess—the month before. Jess had a rehearsal for a concert she was in and couldn't come. Was this what had made her upset? It was not as if we'd done anything particularly special that afternoon. Phoebe cooked us lunch, and when her mother came home from her job at the language school, Phoebe had coaxed her into playing us a Chopin piece on their piano.

I met Richard's gaze.

'Jess has never said anything to me,' I said.

'Oh, she wouldn't.' He gave me a look, which seemed to convey that we both knew she was too proud for that. He put the empty beer bottle on the ground. 'And hey...I know Oliver's being a bit of a prick tonight. To Sean, I mean. Interrupting his story about Japan and everything.'

Peering at him through the half-light, with his crooked smile and long, dark lashes, I remembered again how Jess said he'd cried when they'd first had sex. Phoebe was right: Richard was great. Jess was too hard on him—all the Aitkens were.

'It's probably just about what happened with Angela,' said Richard.

'Angela?' I was confused. 'Did she and Oliver break up or something?'

'Oh no,' Richard bent down and plucked the bottle off the brickwork. 'I mean how Sean tried to kiss her.' Seeing the startled look on my face, he rushed on. 'Not recently! Two years ago. At some birthday thing of her brother's. Don't worry, nothing even happened. It's just that Angela mentioned it to Oliver, and he can't help but have a pissing contest, can he?'

I laughed uncertainly.

'I guess not.'

'There you are.' Jess slammed the freezer door shut as Richard and I walked back into the kitchen. 'I was beginning to wonder where you two had snuck off to.' Her balloon of hair had begun to deflate.

'Caro, be a darling and take this in, will you?' Mrs Aitken handed me a mousse decorated with blueberries in a large crystal bowl. 'Jess helped me make it. Doesn't it look marvellous?'

'All I did was the blueberries,' Jess replied. 'Careful with that bowl,' she warned me. 'It's Mum's favourite thing in the world.'

Mrs Aitken smiled at me confidentially. 'Caro's very responsible,' she said, and I rode the familiar wave of uneasy guilt in the face of her kindness.

I followed Jess back into the dining room. The candles burning on the mantelpiece were almost down to the end of the wick, their long flames making giddy shadows on the wall. The white tablecloth was stained with specks of gravy and wine. Angela Elardo had her shoes off and had draped her pantyhosed legs across Oliver's lap. They were dating and could do such things, of course, but there was something showy about the scene that went against what I knew about her— what I thought I knew, anyway. Perhaps I was overreacting after what Richard had told me.

Sean and the judge were at the other end of the table, and what was immediately clear was that they were both drunk. I had seen Jess's father like this a few times before, but never Sean. Mr Aitken had clearly plied him with more wine since I'd left the room. His eyes swam. His cheeks were flushed, and he was talking.

'In that type of role, you've got to show some integrity,' Sean was saying to Oliver as I re-entered, in a voice louder than usual. 'It's the most powerful role, really, in the world. So hey, keeping it in your pants isn't too much to ask, if you know what I mean.'

I stood listening, uncomfortable but fascinated. Exactly how much wine had he drunk? I wondered if I was seeing the real Sean for the first time. Perhaps my boyfriend was a person of fierce opinion, his calm exterior a mask for a furiously churning soul.

'I think we all know what you mean, Sean,' Oliver said, chin out, giving him a condescending smile.

Jess positioned a placemat in the middle of the table.

'I have *no* idea.'

Sean looked at her with irritation. 'Sexual favours,' he said, emphasising the vowels. 'Blowjobs.'

His deliberate lewdness sent Mr Aitken into a fit of spluttering laughter. Sean grinned. Jess glanced at me and raised an eyebrow. I carefully lowered Mrs Aitken's mousse onto the placemat.

'Completely irrelevant,' Oliver said, stroking Angela's leg in long, deliberate strokes, his eyes on Sean. He reached for his glass of water and took a gulp. 'I'm not saying he's a great president or anything, that's a different discussion. But just because Clinton and Lewinsky were, well—'

'—rooting like rabbits in the Oval Office?' Sean filled in, glancing sideways at Jess's father.

'Even if that's true. It's his private business. So what?'

'So what? Trust you to ask that question, Oliver,' said Sean, just as Mrs Aitken entered the room.

Oliver stared at Sean levelly.

'What's that supposed to mean?'

'Oh, just that you're a bit of a dick,' said Sean, and laughed loudly.

There was a hush. Sean looked around the table with a grin that wavered when he saw Mrs Aitken. She turned smoothly and walked out the way she had come.

The judge gave a throaty cough.

'We might get you some water, kid. Be a love, Jess, and pass us a glass.'

Sean gazed across the table at Angela Elardo, who looked away.

That's when I saw it. Angela. *She* was the reason he was making a fool of himself, trying to one-up this brute of a college boy. I thought about what Richard had said in the garden about the kiss. I looked at Sean's dinner jacket and turtleneck jumper. He wasn't wearing them for me.

Suddenly I wanted to be at home again, my fingers in Skip's fur, my hand against his steady heartbeat.

Instead I watched Sean stare at Angela, and it made me think of my mother again, and how she had looked up earlier from her paper to see whether I had invited Sean inside. She'd been waiting for me to introduce him. Suddenly I understood that she thought I was ashamed of her and her small life, and this had made her critical of my crumpled skirt. It wasn't the only reason she'd been critical: she and my father had worked hard to give me access to a world that they themselves had no access to, and she wanted me to fit in. With my law degree and rich friends, she saw a bright future for me and wanted to protect it.

But that's why I hadn't brought Sean inside to meet her. Seeing us together would have given her hope.

The day I'd gone to Phoebe's house, she'd opened the door and accidentally shut it again in my face.

'What's gotten into you?' I said, laughing as she opened it a second time.

'You make me nervous,' said Phoebe, and shrugged.

It was later, when we were alone in her bedroom, after we'd listened to her mother play the piano, that I told her about Sean: we were going on a date; he would be the first boy I'd been out with.

'You've never had a boyfriend? Why do you think that is?' she asked, her voice light.

'I'm an unattractive bore, I suppose.'

Phoebe reached out to touch my hair.

'Well, that's definitely not it.'

I remembered how it felt—her saying that, doing that. It was not a feeling I'd ever had with Sean, not even the first time we'd kissed. I'd told myself this was because Sean and I were so comfortable with each other. It was a sign the two of us were meant to be together. But looking across at him sitting glassy-eyed at the Aitkens' dinner table, I was beginning to doubt it.

I took the used dessert plates into the kitchen. Richard was there with Mrs Aitken, his hands in a sink of soapy water, washing-up gloves on, the cheery lilt of his voice pedalling furiously into the gulfs between her brief replies.

'Let me do that,' I offered, suddenly desperate to help.

Mrs Aitken gave me a sharp look; it took me by surprise.

'You need to take Sean home, dear,' she said, her mouth tight.

Shame laid a heavy egg in my stomach. My eyes began to sting. This was it, at last—everything I'd dreaded. I wanted to be scrubbed and dried and put away out of sight. Though something—the thought of her husband with his wine-stained teeth perhaps, or her son sliding his hands across his girlfriend's thighs—made me resist.

'I'll be quick.'

Mrs Aitken moved soundlessly to the other side of the kitchen.

'Thanks, Caro,' murmured Richard. 'The cutlery can go in the dishwasher, but you'll have to wash the plates. Water might need a top-up.' He picked up a tea towel.

We worked in silence, aware of Mrs Aitken sorting linen on the bench behind us. Minutes passed. Nothing but the scrape of shifting crockery and the hum of the pool pump outside the window.

'You catching up with Phoebe this weekend?' Richard said at last, breaking the lull. 'I'd love to get her tips on Japan sometime. You know, Jess and I are planning a stopover in Tokyo on our way to Oxford at the end of the year.'

Surprised, I looked up at him.

'You're going to Oxford?'

Richard nodded. 'Jess plans to study there after third year. Our parents are generously sponsoring a reconnaissance trip.' He glanced at Mrs Aitken, smiling graciously.

Jess, who barely put effort into her studies, was going to go to Oxford? I had no idea what to say.

'Pity Phoebe couldn't come tonight,' added Richard. 'I would have liked to see her.'

Mrs Aitken piped up. 'It's a long way for her to travel though, isn't it?'

I cleared my throat. 'Her place is not so far.' I twisted the tap and hot water gushed.

'I guess not,' she replied, looking at me finally. 'It just seems like it sometimes, doesn't it? Is she on the western side, where they built all the new houses? They generally prefer modern houses, don't they?' She bunched her face into a distasteful look. 'No gardens. Lots of blond brick.'

It took me a moment to realise what she was saying. Who *they* were. I thought of Phoebe's mother, her graceful fingers on the piano keys.

I heard a laugh. Looking up from the dishes, I realised it was Richard. He'd turned towards Mrs Aitken, mouth wide. Mrs Aitken was smiling at him conspiratorially.

I turned off the tap and the pipes shuddered.

The smell of chlorine wafted from the garden. My hands in the dishwashing gloves felt unlike my own. I lifted the next item from the bench in a high arc. Richard and Mrs Aitken followed my actions with a curious gaze.

I ignored them. My thoughts were already drifting towards tomorrow. Sean had some plan to take me to the museum, but I doubted that would happen now. I could hear Jess laughing in the living room.

I would call Phoebe in the morning and ask if she was free.

I straightened my arms further. There between my hands, far above the benchtop, the rounded, patterned bottom of Mrs Aitken's favourite crystal bowl shone slick with detergent. From a faraway place I watched it slip from between my fingers. Like a diver into water, it fell onto the polished wood, cracking into tiny shards of light.

Black Sand

Daley Rangi

I

The wind picked up as Kara made her way across the ridge towards the direction of the debris. More and more had washed ashore recently, not that anyone in town would know—or care. She could spy it from the hill, grassy knoll rubbed raw from routine.

The binoculars. The squat. The frown. The rubbish was always there, but a regimen brought comfort. She knew—everyone knew—that the river had long been a dumping ground, once weekly warnings now communal indifference. Barely water (that would imply life), it stretched for kilometres, all the way to the mountain. Anything lost upon this conveyance would soon make its way here, to where the swollen mouth gnawed at the coast. It had once been a game to guess precisely where the roiling froth would deposit the bounty each morning, or even if one would arrive. However, as the months dragged on, and the sea fog thickened, Kara could almost set her watch to the 9.42am low tide. At least something was consistent now. A tiny glob of terror shivered in her belly. No, consistency implied stability.

She pushed down the creeping lump rising in her throat, that sparse canned breakfast on the move. Today it had been a slop of tiny white sausages, the unsure meat of some long-gone livestock. She reminded herself to check the expiry date. What was time anymore but a measure of survival? Brushing lighter thoughts to the fore, and the dirt from her knees, she launched herself down the path. Once trodden by better days, she took great pride in keeping up traditions—a trip too confident this morning. Emboldened by a precious glimpse of blue rummaging through the turgid sky, Kara crunched her toes upon a rock, and tumbled down the slope, rewarded with a mouthful of black sand. Dense, heavy, thick with iron—the kind that sticks to the gums and reminds one of blood.

Kara chewed absent-minded slurs at the particles, relinquishing this moment to the warm embrace. She noticed it had been getting much hotter, much earlier. On especially pungent days, it could be unbearable after ten, which made her expeditions all the more expeditious. Burn blisters tickled her swiftly bruising toes as she dug them deep, callused soles pushing her up and out. A tired salute to the absent sun—the trash goddess has risen once more.

Kara meandered her way across the beach, ducking between enormous piles of wind-eaten, sun-bleached, salt-scented driftwood. She made sure to pick up a good stick to poke at the scraps. Long and sturdy, not too thick but not too brittle, just about head height, with a proper, natural bend. Not a curve, mind you. A knot, nature's handle, about halfway down, wouldn't go astray either. There was no such luck this morning, even with a growing selection to choose from. She remembered a particularly efficient branch from days earlier that had disappeared overnight from the porch. Good sticks appeared to be in short supply. She proposed to keep this one inside.

The wind picked up the drying sand, nipping at her legs and heels. Scurrying towards the flotsam—or maybe jetsam, if she could uncover a guilty party—she held her stick aloft, as though it were a spear, just in case something alive ambushed her from the seaweed. As it turned out, there was no need. As she approached the clump, her prize, she lowered it in disbelief. It couldn't be—not here, not like this. The sea had surely belched up a hoax. Yet no, closer inspection brought Kara only shaking hands and a dawning truth. A salty tear joined the spray, a scream stuck in her throat. The unmistakable shag of brown feathers could not lie.

There, crumpled upon the black sand, lay a dead kiwi.

II

The town—if you could call it that, more a mulling, a milling, a murmuring of humans—was oddly well prepared to receive the news of a deceased national icon. After all, what was another death? Everything dies; or rather, everything was in the process of it. All were content in the rot—there was no resistance, not anymore. Murmurs of apocalypse came and went, as common as the death.

Were they in it?

Was it yet to come?

Was this it?

Is this all there is?

The pervasive stench of demise bore deep in the soul of these denizens. Permission for anyone to die—just do it quietly. In the corner. Yes, there is fine. Don't leave a note. No, no one will read it. Care was now a past participle. Limping, whimpering, towards oblivion.

So even as word swiftly spread, like sandflies to a carcass, and the rumours milled, and the body of the bird rested for a fleeting moment within the dark dankness of Kara's mum's sister's daughter's old chillybin (none of these people were alive anymore, most weren't)—this event was only another speck of dust in the wind.

Kara had tried her best to transport it covertly, to keep it a secret, but both secrets and garbage bags were in short supply, and no match for the long, mighty beak. Nostrils poked through the dry rot of every available sack. She considered removing the beak but was distressed by the prospect.

Why was she so attached to this avian cadaver? Hunger drove all decisions.

She sourced a backpack from a nearby porch that would surely fit such a rotund specimen. After all, she reasoned, if her stick had been stolen, she could take this now. Someone would likely miss this backpack but soon they too would take what they needed. The circle of life, give or take. Stuffing the kiwi into the bag turned her strong stomach, as the flesh and fat jiggled and jostled, though she was careful not to snap the brittle bones.

She crawled her way back up the hill, pack bulging like a tumor. She'd planned the route in her head, a stealthy trip down the road: one left, one right, another right, one fence jump, a leap across the remnants of a river, followed by a second fence jump, one left again, climb three walls of varying heights, then clamber onto a roof—take a deep breath of smog—jump down and strut home like nothing had happened.

Kara would have indeed succeeded, considering how she did it every day, if she hadn't tripped once more, on the very same rock, and if not for that dog, that damned dog that lurked in that damned hut on the edge of this damned coastline. Goddamn, she'd love to eat that dog. If that goddamned delicious-looking dog hadn't appeared, like some scruffy Antichrist. Oh how she'd like to suck the meat from those bones. If it hadn't wrestled the backpack from her with its drooling jaws, and sprinted towards the centre of the town. What was this thing even eating to give it such strong, thick, fleshy-looking legs?

Maybe she could have let it go, but she'd already done that, did that; every minute of every day was an exercise in letting go. Maybe if she hadn't jumped to her feet and chased after it, screaming and wailing at the brute 'Stop, stop, stop, stop—that's mine!', then she wouldn't have run into the main street as it barked and howled joyfully at its catch, ripping the bag open to expose that jiggling, fatty lump. Maybe she wouldn't have tackled it to the ground and bashed its brains out with a deceptively heavy volcanic rock, anger rising inside her like lava, crying up her soul and regurgitating those tiny white sausages onto the pavement. Maybe a group of passersby wouldn't have asked her, 'Are you going to eat that?'

Maybe she wouldn't have spat at them as they dragged the dog's carcass into the shadows. Maybe she wouldn't have cradled that poor, dead, feathery mess in her arms with the whole town staring at the chaos with a shrug before moving on with the tedious task of survival. Maybe she wouldn't have gone to the battered, slightly burnt remains of her cousin's house, and she wouldn't be sat, now, staring, abyss-like, at the insides of her dead mum's dead sister's dead daughter's chillybin.

There, crumpled upon the black sand, lay a dead kiwi.

III

K ara stared up at the mountain; once full of life and lustre, a
peak of white was now dark and despairing. What was the
word for that cold powder again? No, no such thing. Hot sand
mistaken; writhing in the melt of a cool memory. This alpine
ancestor soared above and beyond the tiny scratched window
of the kitchen—shedding shadows as the veiled sun began its
lonely ascent. A picture of a bearded man hung just below the
porthole as if the mountain was his crown. It could have been
any mountain, but this one was hers. It could have been any
man, but this one was hers. Neither were hers alone, they were
family. The immensity of the view felt impossible from this
angle, but sometimes logic is forgiven in the search for beauty.
She wondered if either man or mountain would return to
health. A deep, rattling groan from the bedroom assured her
neither would. Not long now.

Her stomach rumbled and grumbled. She didn't know if
she could keep it down. The filthy memory of this second
breakfast tried to burst through her abdomen. The microwave
had done its best with what remained of the bird. The fat didn't
cook so much as it succumbed, a reluctant surrender to the
radiation. As the digital green ticked down and the meat
shuddered with anticipation, an acrid smoke had filled the air,
the kind that seizes the throat and pricks at the eyes. She would
have cooked it on the stove, but a naked flame could ignite the
air. When had fire ever been a luxury?

At least they still had electricity. Poor woman's fire. At least
this was a meal. At least the mountain was still there, reaching
to her through the glass. She pondered how she should boil the
bones, the beak, how she could attempt to sew the feathers

together into a cloak—no, no, there was not enough for that, but nothing could be wasted anymore. She refused. She wondered if she would be judged for what she had done. She had heard stories that the bird was once eaten by her kin, but none were kindred and stories were now lies, untrustworthy. When had stories ever been a luxury? A naked truth could ignite the air.

She wondered which words were whispered by those people in that language all those years ago, in those once-forests. It could have been any language, but this one was hers. It could have been any people, but this one was hers. Neither were hers alone, they were family. It must have felt so loving to live and hunt under canopy, family wrapping family in a green cloak. Trees were, as all was, a luxury. When had trees ever been a luxury?

A tear threatened to salt the edge of her eyes, as the memories flooded the undergrowth. Not her memories alone, but family, but the fire, but the stories, and the trees.

An ethereal hand gripped her stomach, an escalating urge suddenly overwhelming. Kara fell to the floor, grasping at her abdomen, the tears flowing and a scream growing. The beast could not, would not, rest. A deep, unsettling wave of fear, these primal contractions. The sheer intensity and hostility of the rejection surprised her, as she began to vomit up everything. An outpouring, a downpour, of distress—no dignity in its exit. She began to choke, reaching for help, but help was also a past participle, and it wasn't long before she collapsed onto the rotting wood, a husk unaware of the fruit it bore.

The wind picked up and whistled through the frame of the house, a haunting, empty sigh as the lingering life emptied from it. 10.42am read the clock. An hour meant nothing in the shadow of millennia. A loud boom shook the foundations, an explosion from somewhere in town, smoke rising from the horizon. The mountain no longer had eyes. Distant waves lapped upon Kara; an abyssal whisper rippled through the silt.

There, crumpled upon the black sand, lay a dead kiwi.

Contributors

Jumaana Abdu is the author of *Translations* (Vintage). She is a Dal Stivens Award winner and a Wheeler Centre Next Chapter alumnus. Her work has been published widely, including in *Thyme Travellers* (Roseway Publishing), an international anthology of Palestinian speculative fiction. During the day, she is a medical doctor.

Dominic Amerena is a writer, researcher and educator. His work has been widely published and he has won numerous prizes, grants and fellowships. His debut novel, *I Want Everything*, will be released in 2025.

Alice Bishop is a writer from Christmas Hills, Victoria. Her first collection of short fiction, *A Constant Hum*, is out via Text Publishing. In 2020, she was named a Best Young Australian Novelist by the *Age/Sydney Morning Herald*. She is currently completing a novel.

Behrouz Boochani is an award-winning writer, journalist, filmmaker and human rights defender. His memoir, *No Friend But the Mountains* (Pan Macmillan, 2018, trans. Omid Tofighian), was written during his seven years of incarceration by the Australian government in Papua New Guinea's Manus Island prison. His most recent book is a collection of political writings titled *Freedom, Only Freedom* (Bloomsbury, 2022, trans. Moones Mansoubi and Omid Tofighian).

'Qobad' was first written in Kurdish and then translated by Boochani into Farsi. This story is the first time Boochani's fiction has been published in English, and has been translated by author and scholar Amir Ahmadi Arian.

Ennis Ćehić is the author of *Sadvertising*, a collection of stories published by Penguin Random House in 2022. His writing has been featured in local and international literary magazines including *Meanjin*, *Assemble Papers* and *LUD Literatura*. He lives and works in Sarajevo.

Paige Clark is a Chinese/American/Australian writer living in Naarm. Her first book, *She Is Haunted*, was longlisted for the 2022 Stella Prize, highly commended for the 2022 Barbara Jefferis Award and shortlisted for the 2021 Readings Prize.

Ceridwen Dovey writes fiction and creative non-fiction, and has received an Australian Museum Eureka Award for science writing. Her most recent book of short stories is *Only the Astronauts* (Penguin Random House, 2024).

Kathryn Gledhill-Tucker is a Nyungar technologist, writer and digital rights activist living on Whadjuk Noongar boodjar. Their creative practice uses poetry, speculative fiction and digital tools to explore the history of technology and our relationship with machines.

Erin Gough writes short stories and novels and has been published internationally. Her novel *The Flywheel* won the Ampersand Prize, and *Amelia Westlake* won the Readings Young Adult Book Prize and the NSW Premier's Prize for Young Adult Fiction. She is a previous winner of the *Griffith Review* Novella Project.

Lee Hana has worked in communications for electoral and peace-building projects throughout Asia. Recently, he has written two historical thrillers set in Timor-Leste and a story collection of post-punk science fiction.

Tracey Lien was born and raised in south-western Sydney. She earned her MFA at the University of Kansas and was previously a reporter for the *Los Angeles Times*. She is the author of the internationally bestselling novel *All That's Left Unsaid*.

Lucy Nelson is a writer of fiction and non-fiction living on Dharawal Country. Her work has appeared in *Meanjin*, the *Sydney Morning Herald*, *Southword* and others. Lucy's first collection of short stories is forthcoming from Summit Books.

Daley Rangi is a shapeshifter, a Te Ātiawa Māori artist at large. Joyfully unpredictable, they generate anti-disciplinary works investigating language, memory and injustice.

Josephine Rowe is the author of several story collections, including *Tarcutta Wake* and *Here Until August*, which was shortlisted for the 2020 Stella Prize. She has twice been named a *Sydney Morning Herald* Best Young Australian Novelist, and her debut novel, *A Loving, Faithful Animal*, was a *New York Times* Editors' Choice. 'Tamanu' opens her new novel, *Little World*, forthcoming from Black Inc. and Transit Books in 2025. An earlier version of this story appeared in *Zoetrope: All-Story*.

Aisling Smith won the 2020 Richell Prize for Emerging Writers. Her debut novel, *After the Rain*, was published by Hachette Australia in 2023 and was longlisted for this year's Australian Literature Society Gold Medal. She holds a PhD in literary studies from Monash University and is a digital nomad, loosely based in Naarm.

———

Suzy Garcia is the editor of *Kill Your Darlings* magazine and series editor of *New Australian Fiction*.

Stories for every reader

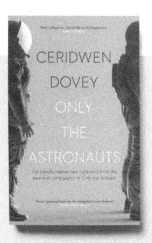

'Ceridwen Dovey has a
rare, wild genius.'
ANNA FUNDER

'A story that is both original
and timeless.'
MELANIE CHENG

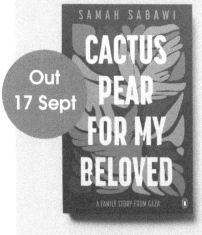

Out
17 Sept

'Samah Sabawi has
written a story of courage
and struggle.' **TONY BIRCH**

'One of the most deeply
considered debuts I have
ever read.' **HANNAH KENT**

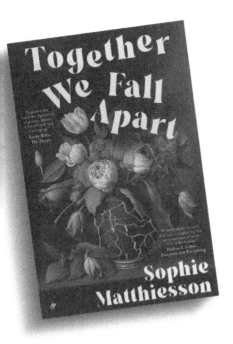

Moving, heartbreaking and devastatingly insightful, *Together We Fall Apart* is a story about running away and coming home.

'I feel weightless. I feel free. It's how I imagine other people feel all the time. And then it's over.'

A dazzling literary debut, *Everyone and Everything* will make you laugh, cry, and call your sister.

SEPTEMBER READS

Every city casts a shadow, where evil flourishes

This memoir offers a backstage pass into life in the chorus – the stars who take their bow from the second row

"A moving work that illuminates the present as much as the past ... a rare treat"
LUCY TRELOAR

Based on his experience as a first responder, Craig sets out a practical game plan to reclaim control, find hope and step into a positive future

SHORT FICTION CRAFT KIT!

JOIN THESE TALENTED WRITERS IN A 5-COURSE MASTERCLASS IN CRAFT:

- Writing Landscape with Alice Bishop
- Crafting Beautiful Sentences with Emily Bitto
- Writing Dialogue with Rebecca Starford
- Voice and Persona with Ellena Savage
- Writing about the Body with Madeleine Watts

FROM $249!

WORKSHOPS.KILLYOURDARLINGS.COM.AU

killyourdarlings.com.au

KILL YOUR DARLINGS

PUBLISHING NEW WRITING EVERY WEEK

'Australia's best cultural and literary journal.'

'Irreverent, with a finger firmly on the pulse.'

'Inclusive, edgy and contemporary, a magazine that inspires readers to become writers.'

'An essential pathway into the Australian literary landscape.'

'Welcoming and accessible online resources and community for writers.'

'A vital mouthpiece for quiet and loud voices.'

'Fearless writing giving voice to a new world.'

—*KYD* READER SURVEY, 2023